Mrs. J. H. Riddell

The government official

A Novel. Vol. 3

Mrs. J. H. Riddell

The government official
A Novel. Vol. 3

ISBN/EAN: 9783337046323

Printed in Europe, USA, Canada, Australia, Japan

Cover: Foto ©Andreas Hilbeck / pixelio.de

More available books at **www.hansebooks.com**

THE
GOVERNMENT OFFICIAL.

A Novel.

IN THREE VOLUMES.

VOL. III.

LONDON:

RICHARD BENTLEY AND SON,

Publishers in Ordinary to Her Majesty the Queen.

1887.

CONTENTS OF VOL. III.

GOVERNMENT OFFICIAL.

CHAPTER I.

WAS IT CHANCE?

SELWYN lay awake almost the whole night, pondering over what had passed. There was much about the matter which he could not understand. He did not comprehend why Mr. Harrison had sent for him, why he should feel or show the smallest interest in what befell him. The evident desire to correct the impression the Chief-Inspector had left was also very puzzling to Selwyn; but, whatever the motive might have been, his common sense told him the advice was good. It was true he had been standing on a precipice. He had almost made up his mind to resign his post, which was fast growing hateful to him, intending not to cast in his lot with the Surveyor, as the latter frequently urged, but to gather up his scanty capital and set out for that New World in which he believed prosperity, if not happiness, lay waiting for any man who sought it with strong arms and a stout heart.

He had been in a dangerous way; but Prudence triumphed, thanks to the spur which Mr. Harrison gave her; and before he went to his office on the following day he resolved to abandon the idea of resignation for the present. Mr. Cramsey found him unwontedly docile, and remarked to Mr. Gough, with a sage shake of the head, he was breaking that young colt in.

' Lord !' he said, ' they're all skittish when they first come under Davey's claws; but he tames 'em, sir.'

' Kerry's tame enough, isn't he ?' said Mr. Gough with a great laugh, ' and it seems to me Serle's one of the same sort. Take care of those claws, Cramsey, else he'll cut yours for you, and your comb too.'

Whereat Mr. Cramsey, much offended, waddled away.

Selwyn had another matter, quite as serious to him, to occupy his thoughts during Mr. Trosdale's absence — Madge. His love for her was no fancy of a moment, but one which had steadily grown for so long, that he was annoyed at his blindness in not having acknowledged it many months before. That she loved him he did not dare to hope, neither was it a question he felt could he ever dare to ask. Knowing how ambitious were the views which Mr. Trosdale entertained for his daughter, as well as for himself, when the profits of the furnace should be harvested, Selwyn conceived he had only one course open to him. It was impossible the Surveyor should wish his daughter to marry a man possessing only a few pounds a year in addition to his official pay ; it was equally impossible that he, with such scanty means, could approach so great an heiress as Madge might become. If she cared for him at all — and sometimes he almost fancied she did—his duty was only so much the plainer. He must leave the house; he would ask Mr. Harrison to obtain an exchange for him into some distant part of the country.

This decision was not arrived at without much sad thought. He felt sorely buffeted by Fortune, poor lad! first involved in troubles which were not of his own making, and now cast out from the quiet haven he had found, to steer his own course on the sea of life. He had no delusions regarding the future; he knew full well the utter loneliness of the existence he was about to accept. It was unlikely, to say the least, that other friends, like the Trosdales, were waiting for him in the strange district to which he might be sent; and even if they were, with what heart could he seek out new acquaintances whilst still yearning for the old?

Kerry found him, on the second day of Mr. Trosdale's absence, lost in thought, and slapped him cheerfully on the back, laughing boisterously when Selwyn started.

'You're getting as yellow as a guinea;

it's my belief you've the jaundice, Serle, and
you won't be well until you get out more.
Come and have some ozone now, on the
Landing Stage. Where's Davey ?'

' Mr. Cramsey's at an appeal meeting,'
said Selwyn peevishly ; 'and I'm quite well,
thank you, Kerry. I'm too busy to come
out.'

' Too cross, you mean,' retorted his friend,
' and that's the truth; for divil a much you've
done since you sat down with those returns.'

' Put it as you like,' answered Selwyn,
' only I'm not coming out.'

Having uttered which ungracious reply,
he began to write, and Kerry went out with
some scornful observation about people who
didn't know when to work and when to play.

At another time Selwyn might have
thought it worth while to follow Kerry and
conciliate him ; but at this moment he felt
his troubles thickening around him too fast
to care whether he had annoyed his friend.
He did not succeed with his work that day,
and left his office rather earlier than usual,
intending to take a walk after having had
his tea. As he let himself into the house

in St. Paul's Square, however, he was met by the servant, who told him Mr. Trosdale had returned quite unexpectedly about an hour before.

'And Miss Madge has gone to get something for his tea.'

'Where is he?' asked Selwyn.

'In the drawing-room, sir.'

Selwyn went upstairs, feeling that the moment had arrived when he must say all he had on his heart.

'Oh, I'm glad you've come,' said Mr. Trosdale. 'Here's a cursed check! Phipps won't look at the furnace unless Hodson approves of it. He is in close relations, it seems, with Hodson, and trusts his own opinion less than his friend's. He says he never looks at new inventions, they must all be dealt with first in London.'

'Did you see anyone else in Sheffield?'

'No one else worth seeing, that I am aware of. Phipps is big enough to buy up every other man in the trade there.'

'Still,' ventured Selwyn, 'a smaller man might have been able to give you a good price for your invention.'

'Pshaw! don't you understand that it's useless to go to a small man with a thing of such magnitude? This furnace will make more than one man's fortune, and it will need a very large capital to push it. If Dick or Tom patronize it, that is of no advantage to me; but six words from Hodson would set the whole thing going.'

'Well, and what do you propose doing now?'

The Surveyor lifted his eyebrows and regarded his young friend as if he thought he had taken leave of his senses.

'I sometimes wonder whether you quite follow me when we talk together,' he said. 'You ask the most foolish questions. What on earth do you expect me to do but go to London?'

'I thought there might be a necessity for your staying here just at present.'

'A necessity? Oh, I understand now. You are thinking of my suspension. I have decided to resign my appointment. Yes,' he went on, with some triumph, as he saw that Selwyn was astonished; 'I have no time now for wrangling with Dandison.

I can occupy myself more remuneratively. I shall write out my resignation to-night. After all, I don't know that this could have happened at a more convenient time. Gad! it's the first thing I've been grateful to Dandison for within my recollection. I should have been sadly embarrassed if I had been tied to the office now.'

At this point they were summoned to tea. Madge was very quiet throughout the meal, and received the news of her father's approaching departure for London without any other comment than an inquiry regarding the number of shirts he would wish to take with him. After satisfying his daughter's anxiety on this point, the Surveyor himself relapsed into silence; and a more unsociable trio could hardly have been found in Liverpool. When Mr. Trosdale rose from table, Selwyn followed him into his room, and began as soon as they were alone.

'I have something to say to you—something which you ought to know.'

'What cursed thing has happened now?' asked his chief; 'have you got into some mischief since I've been away?'

'It's an older story than that; but it's mischief enough for me,' replied Selwyn, trying to speak lightly. 'I see no use in mincing matters——'

'Don't mince them, for God's sake!' interrupted Mr. Trosdale.

'It is only this, then . . . You must try not to be hard with me . . . I have learned to like your daughter too much for my own happiness.'

It was done, the great avowal was made, and Selwyn watched with breathless anxiety its effect on the Surveyor. He did not explode into violent passion, he did not even become sarcastic, and make unpleasant remarks about the means which that man would require who might aspire to woo Madge; instead of doing either of these things, he only said, rather contemptuously, and with an air of relief:

'Is that all? I was afraid something had happened.'

The carelessness of the tone in which he uttered these words was more than Selwyn could stand.

'Do you call that nothing?' he asked

indignantly. ' I wonder what you consider of importance, if this is trifling ?'

The Surveyor waved his hand impatiently.

' Important enough to you, no doubt,' he said ; 'and at any other time I might be interested in the affair. But really I am too busy just at present. I don't see any objection. That's what you wanted to know, I suppose.'

' Do you mean that I have your permission to speak to Miss Trosdale ?' asked Selwyn, overjoyed at his unexpected success.

' Oh Lord ! yes. I thought you had done that. Go and speak to her by all means, and tell me the result at some convenient time, when I am not so much pressed with my own affairs.'

' I'm afraid you think me very inconsiderate.'

' All people are inconsiderate to me,' replied the Surveyor ; after which remark he closed the door behind Selwyn, and devoted himself to writing his resignation.

Selwyn found Madge sitting in the drawing-room. She was sewing—re-making an old dress, that in the weather which was now

upon them was to serve out the third summer
of its existence.   She had seated herself on
a sofa in the window, in order that the light
might fall upon her work, and was looking
really beautiful.   It was not the beauty which
one might expect to see on a girl's face—
not the happy radiance that proceeds from
perfect health and a mind at ease.   It was
a serene peace which illuminated Madge's
countenance, an expression which did not
erase the lines of care, but rather turned
each one of them into an added charm—an
outward sign of the strong spirit within,
which dominated troubles of every kind,
drawing blessing forth from them.

She looked up as Selwyn entered, and said,
as if surprised :

'What, idle !   Does my father not want
you ?'

'I have come to spend the evening with
you, if you will let me,' answered the young
man shyly.   'Do not send me away.'

'Of course, I shall be delighted if you will
stay.   But I don't quite understand why the
attractions of the great invention have failed
to keep you by its side.'

'You talk as if the furnace were alive.'

'I almost wish it were.'

'What do you mean ?   Why ?'

'If it were a live human being that my father had contracted such a fondness for, its keep would certainly be less costly now, and in the time to come——'

'Why do you stop ?'

'Never mind the future,' said Madge, with determination. 'I do not like talking about it.' She laid aside her work, and added, 'Shall I play to you ?'

'Not now.   Talk to me instead.   Or rather, let me talk to you.   I have been thinking a great deal about the future, and, in spite of what you say, I want to tell you all my thoughts.'

He was quite calm now ; the sound of his voice gave him courage.

'I have been thinking that there is change before us, and that this life, which has been so pleasant, so very, very pleasant to me, cannot last for ever.   There will come a time, perhaps before long, when the old home will know neither you nor me any more ; and strangers will go up and down these stairs and live in these rooms, but we shall not be here.'

He stopped, and Madge said:

'Go on. That is not all you have to say.'

'What I want to say is this. I have begun to learn how strong the force of circumstances is in our lives. I don't know whether it is a blind destiny or the hand of God which sometimes shapes out a new course for us so suddenly; but I do know that we cannot resist this invisible power which drives us here and there, and that we can only give way, and take what happiness lies in our reach.'

'Still I do not follow you,' said Madge, very gravely.

'I will tell you. There is change coming towards us; those circumstances which neither you nor I are master of, are preparing at this very moment a new life for us. If I could remain as I am now always, I would do so; but I cannot. Your father is going to London. I know not where his business may take him. He will succeed, and then he will leave Liverpool, taking you with him; but I shall remain behind.'

'All this may be true, but why pry into the future? Is not its evil enough for the day?'

There was a pitiful appeal in the girl's voice, but Selwyn did not heed it.

'Listen to me,' he said. 'I was by the river, watching the gulls, the other day; and there were two which flew up from the water in company, and sailed side-by-side far above me in the air. But they were not really together, and in a few minutes I saw that they were further apart, and presently each went its own way.'

'Well?'

'If they had chosen, they might have remained always together. They need not have parted ever while the world lasted for them. I love you too much to part with you in this way. I cannot pass my life without you; and, when I see you about to drift away, I know the time has come for me to speak.'

Madge did not answer; she sat with her face hidden in her hands; and Selwyn went on :

'You do not know how necessary you are

to me. If I have any strength of purpose, it is you who have given it to me. If I am able to see in their true proportions the things which happen in my daily life, it is you who have helped me to that insight. If I am more earnest, more capable of taking a man's place in the world, I say again, it is to you, and only to you, that I am indebted. You may not know it '—for she made a gesture of dissent—' but it is true. And oh ! my dear, over and above all that, I love you! If you had done me as much harm as you have done me good—yes, if you had done ten times more, I should love you still. It is no boy's fancy. You have changed me into a man ; you have taught me a man's earnestness and a man's love.'

He laid his hand on hers, and remained silent for a moment.

'Do not send me away, Madge,' he said, speaking with a passionate throb in his voice, 'or you will break my heart!'

The girl withdrew her hand from his, and looked him in the face. Her eyes were wet with tears, but she was quite composed.

'You do not know what you are asking,'

she said steadily. 'Oh! do you not see that we are a blighted family, and that what is linked with us can never prosper? You shall not spoil your life. Why did you not go when I warned you so long ago? Oh, it was a miserable chance sent you here!'

'I believe,' answered Selwyn, 'that it was through no accident I came here. What induced the Chief-Inspector to send me to Liverpool? Was it chance? If so, was it chance also that caused me to make my little sketch in the office on that eventful day when your father discovered me? What a series of chances followed after that! His inviting me to come here, my illness, and the understanding which you and I came to. No. Madge; these were no chances. And trust me, my darling, it will be for good. For even if you will not love me, I shall have loved you, and known you, and I must always be better and happier for that, though I shall be unhappy too; but you do love me a little, don't you?'

He drew closer to her, and again laid his hand on hers, which this time she did not withdraw.

'Have confidence in the future, my own,' he said, almost doubting the reality of his happiness. 'If you have not been prosperous in the past, we will work together and be prosperous in the future. I am young and strong and hopeful, and, if I have your love, shall be able to slay dragons. Lay aside your fears. I will take the whole risk, if there be any, only too gladly.'

'You do — you take it all,' whispered Madge; 'it is all giving on your part!'

But that was her last protest ere her thankful lover took her trembling to his heart.

CHAPTER II.

MR. TROSDALE'S VIEWS.

IN an airy sort of way, which might be taken as a jest or as sober earnest, Mr. Kerry had, about ten days after Mrs. Gibbs' party, hinted that it might be only civil if he called in St. Paul's Square and paid his respects to the finest girl he ever saw out of Ireland—or in it, for that matter.

To this tentative remark Selwyn, who was in a very irritable mood, did not respond in at all a good spirit. Disgusted with the snubbing administered by Mr. Dandison, smarting under the rule of Mr. Cramsey, anxious concerning Mr. Trosdale, and troubled as to the chances of his own love-affair, it was natural that he should pooh-pooh Mr. Kerry's suggestion with greater ill-humour than he had ever previously evinced.

The memory of that remarkable evening and of the exhibition in which he had been involved were so hateful to him, that he felt compelled to give his free-and-easy friend a good snubbing. During the whole of their acquaintance Selwyn had never been so nasty nor Mr. Kerry so meek.

It was not in the least necessary, the former authoritatively stated, for the latter to call on Miss Trosdale ; on the contrary, if he did so he would be taking a very great liberty —and much more to the same effect ; which being met by Mr. Kerry with many ' Well, wells,' ' Maybe you're right,' ' To be sure you that has seen the height of fine company ought to know what's the proper thing to do better than a poor devil of a tax-man who has never been asked to put his legs under a decent table since he came to this God-forsaken country,' the battle ended apparently in Mr. Kerry's complete defeat and Selwyn's somewhat remorseful victory.

' After all, the man meant no harm,' he reflected ; ' but it is necessary to be a trifle rough with such people now and then, even for their own good.'

Mr. Serle felt so sure of this that he never attempted to mollify his rather roughly stated decision ; neither did he try to make up in any way for his imperious negative ; therefore it was all the more beautiful on Mr. Kerry's part that he expressed no resentment, but treated Selwyn in precisely the same manner as he might have done had the question never arisen.

He helped the ' snipe ' against his will ; he gave the ' young man ' advice for which the young man was not in the least degree grateful ; he took his part against Mr. Cramsey ; and finally he said one afternoon, shortly before closing time, ' I'll walk a piece of the way home with you, if you have no objection.'

Even if he had objected it would have been difficult for Selwyn to say so ; but, as it happened he was in better spirits than usual, he assented with such readiness to the arrangement that Mr. Kerry, looking at him curiously from the corners of his eyes, remarked :

' I am glad you have got rid of that pain which was troubling you.'

' What pain ?' asked Selwyn.

' In your temper—there is no worse place going to have one ; you are more like the young fellow I took to long ago than I have seen you this many a day.'

' I am happier—perhaps that is the reason.'

' I won't ask you what the devil you have got to make you happier, because if I did you'd maybe answer, " What business is that of yours ?" and, as we're getting on so well, I'd like to keep well.'

' You will know, perhaps, some day.'

' We'll know everything some day in the next world,' returned Mr. Kerry. ' Even, as Erskine said, the reason why boots are always too tight in this.'

' You speak feelingly,' said Selwyn ; ' are your boots too tight ? I see they are new.'

' They are new, young man, but they are not tight——'

'And you are dressed *à quatres épingles*— are you going out to spend the evening ?'

' Never mind where I am going—" you will know some day." '

Even then no suspicion crossed Selwyn's mind concerning Mr. Kerry's destination—so, talking much as usual, they at last arrived in St. Paul's Square, where Mr. Serle stopped and bade his friend good-evening.

'I'll walk with you to the door,' said Mr. Kerry.

'Oh! I won't take you so far out of your way,' returned Selwyn, full of consideration.

'It is all in my way,' answered Mr. Kerry, and Selwyn could offer no objection, though greatly wondering where Mr. Kerry was going.

As they neared the Surveyor's door Madge was crossing from St. Paul's. At sight of the Irishman she hurried her pace a little, and came forward smiling as Selwyn had never seen her smile on him—and it was with much ado he could keep from assaulting Mr. Kerry when that individual said :

' Here she comes, the darling of the world —look at her !'

Selwyn did look at her. He was a very simple, straightforward, and affectionate young fellow, and the ways of women were utterly strange to him.

If Madge, the wise, the prudent, the enigmatical, his promised wife, had adored Mr. Cramsey's Assistant her greeting could not have been more cordial.

'Oh! Mr. Kerry,' she said, 'I was afraid you had forgotten me.'

'I could never do that,' said Mr. Kerry, most seriously in earnest.

'At all events, your promise to come and see me,' returned Madge with a roguish laugh.

'I'll never forget anything my life long that concerns you,' declared Mr. Kerry.

'After that pretty speech I must give you some tea,' said Madge, sweeping a little curtsey, and then they all passed into the dining-room, where Mr. Trosdale greeted the Irishman in a genial and familiar manner, and asked 'if the tax-offices were still in the same old place.'

'Indeed, and they are,' answered Mr. Kerry; 'and the same old people in them; but I am mistaken if there won't be some changes after a bit—maybe Davey himself will have to move his laundry.'

'It was an accursed hole,' said Mr. Trosdale, referring to the tax-offices.

'It is good enough for me, perhaps because I know no better,' remarked the Irishman in a tone which made everyone except Selwyn laugh. 'It seems strange, though, to be there without you; and I dare say you feel it strange to be here without us. Now don't you?'

'Should you care to know exactly how I do feel?' asked Mr. Trosdale.

'I should; though I am much afraid from your manner your feeling is not over-pleasant.'

'I don't see how it should be,' answered the ex-Surveyor. 'After the many years I have spent in the office—years simply cut out of my life—I feel like a prisoner too late released, a captive into whose flesh the chains of his captivity have eaten, but who is thankful for his enfranchisement on any terms.'

'Lord bless me!' exclaimed Mr. Kerry, whose volubility was for the moment completely swamped by this deluge of eloquence.

'You, I dare say, know nothing of such a feeling,' observed Mr. Trosdale, pleased with the effect he had produced.

'Heaven be praised, I don't!'

'I should not have thought such content a

thing worth praising heaven for,' returned Mr. Trosdale contemptuously ; 'but if you are satisfied I may be.'

'Oh, it's easy enough for a poor drudging fellow like myself to be satisfied,' replied Mr. Kerry with mock humility. 'I have no chance of ever making anything except in the service. You are altogether different. You have had the luck to make a fortune ; and I'm sure I wish you health to enjoy and wisdom to spend it.'

'You are very kind—but perhaps you will be good enough to explain how you came to imagine I had made a fortune.'

'If there's any secret about the matter,' said Mr. Kerry, answering the ex-Surveyor's tone more than his words, 'I am sure I'm sorry I spoke—but it's common talk ; old Davey has been running about the office open-mouthed.'

When Mr. Kerry said this Selwyn looked straight at Mr. Trosdale, but Mr. Trosdale would not look at him.

'How Mr. Cramsey could know anything about the matter I am unable to guess,' replied the ex-Surveyor ; 'and his statement is incorrect. I have not made my fortune.'

'Well, you are in the way of making it, anyhow.'

'I trust so,' answered Mr. Trosdale stiffly. To him it seemed a sort of desecration that his approaching wealth should be so lightly spoken of—as if it had come of itself without the help of his own enormous labour and vast knowledge.

'Cramsey says there is no doubt about the matter. You've got a notion of a new sort of fire-stove, haven't you?'

'Fire-stove!' repeated his host, in the tone of a man who mentally added, 'And this is fame!' 'It is to be hoped the next time your chief interests himself in my affairs he will at least take the trouble of being accurate.'

'Sure you needn't care what he is—those that win may laugh—and Davey was nearer crying than laughing when he told Gough you were off to London to get your first instalment. I hope you had a pleasant time there. How were they getting on at Somerset House?'

'I do not know, sir, and I do not care,' retorted Mr. Trosdale. 'I wish never to hear of Somerset House nor taxes again.'

'Faith, and there's many will agree with you there,' said Mr. Kerry. 'I like taxes myself—they are meat and drink to me ; and why wouldn't they be, as they are my living ? But to a man that can't meet them they're battle, murder, and sudden death all in one.'

It was in this manner conversation proceeded during tea. Mr. Trosdale was not an easy man to talk to. His mental corns were so numerous it was difficult to avoid treading on some of them—for which reason it was only when he had the field to himself things ever went smoothly for many minutes at a time —and everyone felt relieved when, the meal being finished, Madge suggested that they would be more comfortable upstairs.

As they passed out Mr. Trosdale touched Selwyn on the shoulder, and said, 'I want you.'

Therefore Madge and Mr. Kerry proceeded to the drawing-room alone.

Just for a few minutes her lover heard the sound of the piano, as she played that mad tarantelle of Heller's, which, indeed, is the chief of all tarantelles. Then he became too much absorbed in Mr. Trosdale's communication to hear Madge's music had stopped, and that she only dreamily struck a chord at intervals that grew longer and longer, till at last her hands fell from the keys, and she sat listening to Mr. Kerry's maunderings, which enlightened her fully concerning all her father had cast aside.

Poor girl! poor girl! She made no comment, but as she sat with her head bent and her heart aching, she could not but remember that old fable about the dog who, seeing the meat reflected in the water, dropped the piece he held in order to seize the shadow.

His life, her life, her mother's life, had been a long famine in consequence of his delusion; everything that makes existence valuable, noble, happy, had been cast under the wheels of a Juggernaut as cruel and relentless as any that ever left a trail of dead and dying creatures behind it.

She was too sad for tears, too hopeless for speech. She did not feel angry, as she had once done. Her heart was soft enough as she looked upon the past as one might look upon it from another world. Whatever the future might hold of evil she and her father would

have to face together.   She saw she could
not avert misfortune and save him.   Her
only dread was that Selwyn might go down
with them if she let him link his fate with
hers ; and yet if she did not——

Lord ! how sweet that love-dream had
been.   If she never understood before, she
understood then.

And almost at the same moment Selwyn
was coming to a fuller comprehension of all
she must ever be to him.

' I am going to be perfectly frank with you,
Serle,' began Mr. Trosdale, as soon as he
had closed the door behind Madge and Mr.
Kerry.

If Selwyn had known more of the world he
would have been aware that such a preface
means the very reverse of what it implies.

' I shall treat you with entire confidence,'
said the ex-Surveyor, as if his first sentence
had not been sufficiently explicit ; ' but I must
ask you to consider the communication I am
about to make as strictly between ourselves.'

' I shall mention it to no one,' answered
Selwyn.

' Not even to Madge, at present,' added
Mr. Trosdale.

'If you do not wish me to tell her, I shall certainly respect your wishes ; still——'

'I do not wish her to know, because then other persons would know, and the consequences prove disastrous.'

'You may depend on my silence,' said the young man unsuspiciously, 'till you give me leave to speak.'

'The fact is——' replied Mr. Trosdale—and then he paused, as if he did not find the end of his sentence quite easy. 'The fact is,' he repeated, finding no help came from Selwyn, 'I find it necessary to go to London.'

'So soon again ? How long do you think you shall be away ?'

'I do not intend to return.'

'At all ?'

'Never at all, I hope. I trust I shall never see Liverpool again. There is not a brick in its houses, there is not a stone in its streets, I do not detest. I have passed long years—miserable years—in it, and I only wish I could blot the recollection of them out of my heart !'

He spoke with a passion which, though

from frequent repetition it did not touch Selwyn as it had once done, still stirred his heart, as such utterances always do stir the young and generous—but, at the same time, he was conscious of a heavy aching pain on his own account. Mr. Trosdale's trouble lay behind, his lay before. If her father left Liverpool, Madge must leave too—while he, Selwyn, would have to remain behind. Then would come the first serious separation. He could not face the full truth at first, but sat like one stunned.

He would be here, she there—and only those that love can tell the full bitterness of the separation that lies between those words.

'Yes,' went on Mr. Trosdale, finding he did not speak; 'I shall feel thankful to quit Liverpool, though I should scarcely have gone yet, had it not been forced upon me.'

'And when?' asked Selwyn. He could not make his sentences any longer. He had to moisten his dry lips before he could say even so much.

'As soon as I can make my arrangements. I shall take Madge with me, ostensibly to give her a little change, and after a short time will explain I mean to reside permanently in London. I want to avoid all leave-takings—all gossiping and discussion of my affairs.'

' I suppose it is quite necessary for you to go?' said the stricken lad wistfully. He had known the blow must come some day, but never thought it would come so soon—oh! not nearly so soon!

Mr. Trosdale, who was smoking, knocked the ash off his cigar the while he looked at Selwyn with irritable astonishment.

'What a question!' he exclaimed. 'Of course it is necessary—nothing could be more necessary. I cannot make out why it seems utterly impossible to drive even a faint idea of the enormous importance of this affair into your head—you are almost as stupid as Madge, though happily not quite so grossly prejudiced. Other people can see the matter in its true proportions. But I suppose I ought not to complain; it has been so from the beginning, and will be so to the end. A prophet is not without honour, save in his own country and among his own people.'

' Indeed you are mistaken, Mr. Trosdale,

if you think I do not appreciate you,' answered unhappy Selwyn.

'Whether,' went on Mr. Trosdale, with a judicial air, 'it is worse to be born blind, or, seeing, voluntarily to remain blind, I cannot pretend to decide—the result is the same. But you are still young, Serle, and in your own interest I earnestly advise you to shake off that narrow habit of mind a Government office always engenders. Now just listen, my good fellow, to a letter I received this afternoon, and contrast the large view, the great grip of mind, with your own petty gropings after paltry details.'

Having delivered himself of which little commination service, he fumbled in his pocket, muttering impatiently as he drew forth first one envelope and then another, which did not prove to be what he expected.

'Tut—that's from Dandison, treacherous hound ; Hope — Stewart — Blake — bills — bills. Pshaw! Ah! here it is. Now listen with all your ears, Serle. This is from——'

Mr. Trosdale, apparently thinking better or worse of the matter, did not say who it was from, but spread out the letter on his knee, and read :

' " It seems to me of the greatest importance that you should arrange to reside in London without any delay. I suggested this, you know, when we parted, and I now urge it more strongly. Hodson is still away, but there is much that can be done while waiting for his return. I see more clearly than ever that your furnace is going to be a big thing, and I urge you not to let any supine delay mar the prospect of a huge success. Success of such magnitude I take to be very much a matter of promptitude." '

At this point Mr. Trosdale paused and raised his head, as if to assure himself that Selwyn was attending. Satisfied on this point, for Selwyn was listening with all his ears, he read on, emphasising every word as if he felt he had at last come to the important part of his letter—

' " You know," this is what my friend says, " you gave me a certain amount of authority to act for you" (I did—that is quite true), " so I have half engaged lodgings for you in Frith

Street, Soho, and if I hear, as I shall hope to hear, that you are coming up at once, I will complete the bargain. You won't do much better. The landlady is clean and honest—she comes from Thorpe-Constantine and I know some of her people——" '

At this point, which certainly was not the end of that important epistle, Mr. Trosdale stopped and placed it carefully in his pocket, saying as he did so :

'There is more in the letter, but nothing material to this issue.'

'Shall you take those lodgings ?' asked Selwyn, who was trembling as if he had come in out of the cold.

' I have taken them,' returned Mr. Trosdale. ' I telegraphed at once to my friend that I would take them from the first of next month.'

' Only a week ahead,' commented Selwyn.

' Only a week ahead, thank God !' repeated Mr. Trosdale, in a tone of repressed triumph. ' I have told Madge she must for once take a holiday, and she will be ready. ' And now to come to what I want you to do—you will help me, won't you ?'

'So far as I can,' answered Selwyn, not very enthusiastically.

'You can help me greatly. Stay on here till I find a way to get rid of this house. Know nothing about me, except that I have gone to London on business of importance, and that the time of my return is uncertain. I want to keep my mind clear to attend to the furnace, and any confounded worry connected with this place might upset me altogether. You understand.'

'Oh yes !' answered Selwyn, but he did not in the least.

'I think that is all I had to say,' remarked Mr. Trosdale, with the air of a man who felt a good evening's work was finished, adding as a sort of afterthought : 'You have laid me under another obligation, Serle—but I shall be able to repay you all soon.'

It somehow happened that Mr. Harrison's visit to Shropshire was prolonged by several weeks beyond the limits he had assigned to it. There was a pleasant party staying in the house, including some old friends of his, all of whom united with the host in searching for every pretext which might defer his departure.   He himself was not unwilling to linger.   And it thus happened that he did not return to town until the middle of the month following that in which he had visited St. Paul's Square.

As he crossed the square of Somerset House on the morning after his arrival he was stopped by the Secretary.

'Ha! Harrison, I didn't expect you for some days yet.   Tut, man, the rain in London would have got on very well without you for a while.   I'm off myself to Inverness on Friday, and don't mean to return a day sooner than I can help.'

'That's all very well for you,' said Mr. Harrison, smiling.   'When I am Secretary I shall extend my ideas of leave.   Being as I am, I think a month in a year quite enough.'

'Gad! I never thought so, even when I was an underling in the Treasury.   So you failed to bring Trosdale to reason?   How was that?'

'Failed.   I did, certainly ; but how comes it you know that?   I have some hopes still.'

'Then you are not aware he has resigned?'

'Resigned ?' Mr. Harrison repeated the word in a tone of such dismal surprise that the Secretary burst into laughter.

'There, I see you know nothing about it,' he said. 'While you were in Shropshire the whole thing has been settled here. Of course, I should have done nothing without seeing you; but the man sent in his resignation, and a very stiff letter with it, so worded there really was only one course left open : we were forced to accept. I managed to get his pension through all right. I had some difficulty about it, though, for I fancy the case really was a questionable one.'

'Poor Martin !' said Mr. Harrison. 'I am afraid he has acted rashly.'

'The man's behaved like a damned ass !' replied the Secretary; 'but I suppose he knows his own business best. Dine with us to-night, Harrison—we are quite alone— and tell Lady Adela all you saw in Shropshire.'

But Mr. Harrison excused himself on the plea of a prior engagement.

Later in the day he sought out Mr. Dandison. That gentleman he found enjoying a steak and a pint of porter in the seclusion of his own comfortably furnished room.

' I'm glad to see you back, Mr. Harrison,' observed the Chief-Inspector. ' Do you mind my going on with my luncheon ? I understood you had returned ; and I presumed you would like to see the papers in the case of your friend Trosdale ; but I have been too much occupied to bring them up. You will find them on the slab of my desk. No, not those—the larger bundle.'

' Thanks,' said Mr. Harrison ; 'if I shall not be in your way I will look at them here.'

' Not in the least. You may find something which needs explanation.'

As he read the papers Mr. Harrison could not but admit that Trosdale had been wholly in the wrong. The letters addressed to him were courteous, and, under the circumstances, forbearing. His replies, on the other hand, were characterized by a tone of irritation which was certainly unfitting in a man addressing his official superiors. It was a hopeless case. Throughout the correspondence it was plain that there could be only one result ; and, critically as Mr. Harrison scanned it, he found nothing which supplied him with a ground for quarrel with Mr. Dandison.

' I feel very sorry about the matter,' remarked the latter affably when his colleague laid the correspondence down. ' It is always painful to see a useful career terminated in this way.'

' Yes ; and I am afraid there are more tangible reasons for regret in this case—for there can hardly fail to be somewhat bitter poverty.'

' Are you quite sure of that, Mr. Harrison ?' asked the Chief-Inspector with a meaning smile.

' As sure as I can be of anything.   May I ask why you doubt it ?'

' I don't doubt anything you are positive about.   But, if you are not sure, I may tell you that, in going up and down the country with my eyes and ears open, I hear many scraps of intelligence ; and I don't think I am beyond the mark in stating that Trosdale has considerable savings.'

' There is some mistake, I fear.   Trosdale is certainly a poor man.'

The Chief-Inspector shrugged his shoulders.

'That depends on the standard you set up,' he answered. 'We are all poor men here; but yet, those of us who have lived prudently own a few pounds, put away in the foot of a stocking somewhere; and I am far from blaming Trosdale for having lived economically. His daughter may thank him now for any little privations she has had to endure. A small house in an unfashionable quarter, with a somewhat reduced household, is not a high price to pay for ease now that a crisis has come. I am tolerably certain of the correctness of what I say, Harrison. More than one person in Liverpool will tell you the same.'

Though the idea was quite new to him, it did not seem improbable to Mr. Harrison. Trosdale could not be living up to his income in St. Paul's Square; the money must have gone somewhere, and he had no grounds whatever beyond his own suspicions for saying it had been frittered away in unprofitable experiments. It was by no means unlikely the Surveyor had been laying money by—that would account easily enough for the hot-headed, independent temper in which he had treated the matter of his suspension.

'I can't say you are wrong, Dandison,' observed Mr. Harrison, rising from his seat. 'I · hope, with all my heart, that you are right.'

'I am pretty sure of it.'

And with that the two men parted, Mr. Harrison returning to his own room, where he at once wrote to Madge, expressing his regret at her father's resolution, and his anxiety to know whether there was still any way in which he could serve her.

The answer, which arrived by return of post, was very brief. It thanked him for his kindness in a few words, which evidently came from the heart of the writer, and assured him that there was no way in which he could aid her father, who did not in fact stand in need of assistance of any sort.

It was not in Mr. Harrison's nature to take offence on any save the strongest grounds; but he felt some annoyance. It was not only that his old friend had taken in the most hasty way what he conceived to be a fatal step ; but he felt that he himself had not been dealt with quite openly. Trosdale might as well have told him he had money laid by; the time had been when nothing would have been kept secret by the one friend from the other. And the solicitude he had shown for Trosdale's interest would have warranted the confidence. However, he had not done so, and now there seemed to be no alternative but to leave him to his own way.

He wrote another note to Madge ere long, begging her to communicate with him if she was ever in any difficulty or trouble, and had no competent adviser near at hand.

This letter Madge did not answer. It reached her on the morning of the day on which she left her home in Liverpool, for a time only, as she imagined, but, as it proved, for ever.

It would be hard to analyze the motives which determined Mr. Trosdale to take his daughter to London with him. He was not wont to show any desire for her company; and she was as much surprised as Selwyn at hearing that she was not to remain behind with Mrs. Graham, as was usual during her father's absences from home. Mr. Trosdale had not, in fact, any clear grasp of his own mind at this time. His faculties were concentrated wholly on the furnace; any question which bore, however remotely, on that topic, he would consider rationally and temperately, but beyond that point all was chaos. His actions in other matters were determined by impulse; his opinions on other subjects were in abeyance. If he had been asked what he thought of his daughter's engagement, he could have given no intelligible answer, save a peevish expression of impatience at being troubled. It was an evident annoyance to him that Selwyn should have chosen this particular time to allow his feelings to become too much for him, and he said bluntly, more than once, that he was disappointed at finding his young friend so incapable of appreciating the relative importance of events.

At first irritable speeches, such as these, had absolutely no effect on Selwyn; they failed utterly to pierce the atmosphere of perfect happiness in which he moved. It was, with him, one of those rare periods in life when all the common objects of existence seem tinged with gold and rose, when the past is flushed with the reflexion of present happiness, and the future way stretches out across a land which only smiles and tempts the traveller onward. Every care was thrust aside ; anxiety for the future he had none. He was perfectly happy ; and if he was conscious of a wish ungratified, it was that the hours might not speed past so quickly, but leave him more time to taste his joy.

It was a sore breach in this elysium when it was decided that Madge should go to London. Madge did not discuss the matter with her father, or offer the least opposition, but at once began to make her preparations.

'You will get on very well alone, Serle, I suppose ?' said Mr. Trosdale, on the evening before his departure.

'I suppose I shall,' answered Selwyn, who felt that the iron had entered into his soul.

But an hour afterwards, finding Madge alone in the drawing-room, he began pleading to her so passionately not to forget him, that Madge was quite dismayed.

'Listen, Selwyn,' she said. 'I cannot tell

you exactly when I shall return. I don't know why my father is going to London, or how long he means to stay. The future is dark before me, and I try not to look into it even so far as a week in advance. Be patient, my dear boy, and trust me that I shall wish for our meeting as much as you. It may be very soon; but if it is long, remember that my place is with my father, and that you do not really wish me to neglect him.'

And very early next morning she was gone.

CHAPTER III.

MR. KERRY IS UPLIFTED.

SELWYN was left alone in the house in St. Paul's Square, out of which had come such potent influence on his life, when Mr. Trosdale and Madge had departed, and an intermittent correspondence was the only link that bound him to them. He felt the loneliness of his position deeply, the shadow of abandonment upon the old home which could never be removed.

At any moment he was able to recall the aspect of the now deserted rooms on a hundred days and evenings in the past—could hear Madge playing on the old familiar piano, and see the Surveyor staring gloomily at the fire with his hands clasped behind his head. But it was always at some past remembrance that these figures sprang into life before his eyes; never could he imagine them in the same well-known attitudes in the time to come.

Mr. Trosdale's letters, too, were rare and meagre in the extreme; he could not gather from them what success his late chief was meeting with; and Madge's epistles, exhaustive as they were, contained no information on this point, about which it was obvious that she knew nothing.

It was a dreary thing to go about the house, contrasting its abandoned aspect with the pleasant air of habitation it had worn in former days. To do so weighed on Selwyn's spirits to such an extent that he restricted himself at last to two rooms on the ground-floor, and hardly ever entered any of the others.

Here then he lived for some time after Mr. Trosdale's departure, working hard and late at his office, and advancing with rapid strides towards a mastery over his work. His leisure hours were spent in preparing for the qualifying examination which every Assistant-Surveyor has to pass before his appointment is ratified. He found that he had still much to do before he could be in such a state of preparation as to present himself before his examiners without a qualm; and he had set his heart on passing a brilliant examination, not only because he understood that the result would determine his seniority, but also because he saw in that an opportunity of recovering some of the ground he had so unfortunately lost with Mr. Dandison.

The time was short : he had already received a warning that early in the autumn he was to be called up for examination, after which, if successful, he would receive the parchment commission from the Treasury which should 'constitute and appoint' him 'to be a Surveyor of Taxes, with full power and authority to do and execute all such matters and things as are by any Act of Parliament appointed to be done and executed by a Surveyor, and generally to act as such Surveyor.'

This summons had arrived earlier in Selwyn's case than was usual, the Board of Inland Revenue being, as Mr. Kerry put it, in the position of the man who had spread a feast and (through the Civil Service Commissioners) invited guests, but yet found half the seats vacant at his banquet. Selwyn had expected that another six months at least would be allowed to him for preparation. He was, however, thanks to Mr. Kerry, fairly well equipped, and under the tuition of the Surveyor who had replaced Mr. Trosdale he was fast becoming qualified to take sole charge of a district.

Mr. John McClosky, who now sat in Mr. Trosdale's seat, was in almost every respect the opposite of his predecessor. He came from Glasgow, and was consequently a member of a nation Mr. Trosdale, notwithstanding the Scotch need for furnaces, despised with his whole heart. Mr. McClosky had a vast capacity for work, was most precise in his dress, punctual in his attendance at the office, chary of his words, never swore nor showed impatience, and yet managed speedily to get the work into order.

It was a matter of complete indifference to a man of Mr. McClosky's energy whether he had a clerk who was acquainted with the work or not ; and he summarily dismissed both the men Mr. Cramsey had introduced, replacing one of them with a short, sallow individual, who was of his own nationality, and who, like his employer, wore a blue ribbon in his buttonhole.

From this time a new order of things was instituted in Third Liverpool. Confusion and untidiness disappeared as if by magic under Mr. McClosky's touch. The dusty piles of paper, of which no one knew the contents, that adorned the corners of the office in Mr. Trosdale's time, were all neatly docketed and stowed away in order. There was no longer any noise or confusion in the office ; each person had his appointed work, and was expected to do it without discussion. Least of all was there any profane swearing, which was a thing greatly abhorred by the new Surveyor; and when a week or two after his arrival Mr. Kerry entered jauntily, his thumbs in the armholes of his waistcoat, and burst at once into his usual salutation : ' Well, Mr. McClosky, how's the bloddy tax ?' the gentleman addressed laid down his pen, and turning round in his chair so as to face the delinquent, inquired sternly :

' Have you no fear of hell-fire in your hairt, Mr. Daniel Kerry ?'

' Lordsake !' ejaculated the astonished Mr. Kerry. 'Why do ye ask me a question like that for ?'

' Let me tell you,' replied Mr. McClosky, in a perfectly unimpassioned voice, 'that there's sure Scripture warrant for believing that they who go forth in the streets uttering profane oaths, and thereby polluting their tongues, which were meant to utter godly words, will be scorched with the hottest flames in the life to come.'

With which words Mr. McClosky resumed his work, taking no further notice of Mr. Kerry, who slunk away quite thunderstricken at this reception of a remark to which he attached no more meaning than to an inquiry touching the state of the weather.

' May I die if he didn't talk as if no one knew anything about hell-fire except himself,' grumbled the Irishman on the same evening to Selwyn, as they sat in the parlour immediately below Miss Dormer's sanctum. ' Who's he, to be so mighty particular ?'

' Well, really, you know,' returned Selwyn,

' "bloddy" is not a word in common use even in tax-offices.'

' I don't care if it isn't. It's a good word, it's short, and it means a lot. What more do you want in a word ?—tell me that !'

'Oh, it's short enough,' replied Selwyn, ' and it's expressive, as you say. But still, I'm not altogether surprised that Mr. McClosky didn't like it.'

' Those Scotch are so mealy-mouthed,' mused Mr. Kerry. 'Why, a hot potato 'd blister them. It comes of drinking that poison they call Scotch whisky, as if there could be more than one whisky, and that Irish.'

Selwyn was accustomed to find that his friend became somewhat intolerant when the merits of Irish whisky were uppermost in his mind, and he therefore brought the conversation into a safer channel by inquiring :

' Have you heard of any promotions lately ?'

' There isn't any more to hear of until I hear of my own. They've given Barnstaple to Webb, and I'm next on the list.'

' Are you, indeed ? Then you may be promoted any day.'

'That's what Dandison said. Faith, I'll be a rich man then, and able to do what I like.'

'Within limits, I suppose. Your salary will not be boundless. For instance, you wouldn't be able to keep hunters on it.'

'Who wants them?' replied Mr. Kerry loftily. 'But I'll get a tricycle, and you can do everything with that that you can with a hunter, bar jumping gates and hedges, which isn't safe at any time. No, my boy, what I mean is I'll be my own master, so that I can shut up my office when I like, and go courting.'

'So, then, you're in love. You didn't tell me that.'

'Who's in love?' demanded Mr. Kerry. 'It's just a way of speaking—everybody understands it. If any one's in love, maybe it's you yourself, though you are not much like a lover.'

To which last statement Selwyn agreed; and then, fearing to be questioned further, he took leave of his friend and went home, pleading a headache.

This conversation is merely a sample of many which took place about this time, when the two friends spent an evening together. Mr. Kerry was, in fact, not quite easy regarding the part he had played during the inquisitorial visit of the Chief-Inspector ; and he had never ventured to tell Selwyn of his interview with Mr. Dandison, rightly judging that his friend would have strongly resented such an attempt to force him out of the connection in which he had chosen to involve himself. Like most people who have meddled in the lives of others, Mr. Kerry began to find, when it was too late, that he had assumed a vast responsibility, and to wish he had allowed his friend to steer his own course, even though it took him on the rocks. As, however, this was now impossible, he was impelled to make what amends he could by seeking Selwyn more than usual, and by urging him constantly to spend the evening in his rooms. This Selwyn was very well inclined to do, for apart from his liking for the Irishman, he was well aware that he benefited largely by the latter's shrewd views of official matters, and his large experience of tax work.

In his preparations Selwyn also obtained great assistance from Mr. McClosky, who was an excellent tutor.   He was pleased to approve of his Assistant's conduct, and seeing the young man punctual in the mornings, and zealous in his work, sent off a glowing report of him to Mr. Dandison, embellished with a quotation from Burns, and devoted himself as far as the extreme pressure of work would allow him to storing Selwyn's mind with all kinds of knotty points which had presented themselves during the course of his long practical career.

> ' The mither may forget the child
>   That smiles sae blithely on her knee,'

he said one morning, at the end of a long and learned discourse upon tithes.   ' D'ye know that song, Mr. Serle ?'

' I do not,' answered Selwyn, adding cautiously, ' do you think the sentiment is true ?'

' True, man ! We've the Bible, to say nothing of our own poet, for it. " The mither,"—that's " mother," you know—" may forget the child," ' and Mr. McClosky swung his forefinger slowly in the air to emphasize the rhythm, ' " that smiles sae blithely on her knee." It's just what children do. " But

I'll ne'er forget—thee, ne'er—ne'er—forget thee, ne'er——" "Tammie" is it ? Well, well! I declare I've forgotten how the verse goes. But that'll show you what a lovely poem it is, and ye'll not find another like it in the wide world. And the application of it is this, Mr. Serle. If ye once get the doctrine of tithes into your head you'll never forget it.'

'I hope not, indeed,' said Selwyn, 'for it has been a tough job to learn it.'

'Ye may say that. And ye may add this, that not ten men in the sairvice understand it ; and that's why they get so befuddled when they're set down in a country district with no one to counsel them. Now you keep what I've told you clear in your head, and ye'll see the whole scheme of country assessments as plain as noonday.'

As Mr. McClosky said this the office-door opened and Mr. Kerry entered. Not with his usual careless gait, however, but drawn up to his full height, and with such an elated expression on his countenance as one might expect to see on that of a General who has just witnessed the success of his own strategy.

'Aweel, aweel! what's the matter with the

man ?' exclaimed Mr. McClosky. 'Are ye going to be married, Mr. Daniel Kerry ? or is a great fortune left to you, that you come in looking like that ?'

'Don't be shouting at me,' said Mr. Kerry loftily, 'or poking fun at me either. I've come to tell you I'm promoted, and I'm a Surveyor myself now.'

Selwyn sprang up and seized his friend's hand.

'My dear fellow, I congratulate you,' he said. 'When did you get the news ? Why didn't you come in here earlier ?'

'Hear him !' said the newly-appointed Surveyor to Mr. McClosky ; 'see how impatient these young chaps are! It's all fire and fury with them, just as if there wasn't a minute to lose.'

Mr. Kerry said this with an air of great dignity.

'Hoot, toots !' exclaimed Mr. McClosky, 'ye know all young people are foolish. And ye're no that old yourself, Mr. Kerry, though it has pleased Providence to make you a Surveyor.'

'It wasn't Providence, man,' objected Mr.

Kerry. ' It was Dandison—long life to him !
—to say nothing of my own merits,' added
the Surveyor modestly.

'Where are they going to send you,
Kerry ?' interposed Selwyn quickly. 'Are
you to have your district at once ?'

' No ; I'm to be at Somerset House,' Mr.
Kerry replied, ' ready to give them advice
when they want it.'

Mr. McClosky smiled, a superior kind of
smile, as if he doubted mightily whether any
one who knew his business would go to Mr.
Kerry for counsel.

' As to that,' he observed, ' you'd best bide
a bit, and make out where ye are, before
offering advice to anybody. There's no way
young men spoil their fortune so fast as trying
to force their opinions on men who might be
their grandfathers. Old men don't like it—
and they're right.'

Mr. Kerry sniffed.

' By the time a man's old enough to be my
grandfather, he's too old for his work,' he
said. ' I'd have all old men bundled out of
the offices, and set aside a wing of Somerset
House for them, and let Government provide

them each with a basin of gruel twice a day and a red woollen comforter every winter. And then, with the terrace to walk up and down on, they'd soon catch cold and die, and make way for their betters.'

'You're a very foolish young man,' said Mr. McClosky, regarding this in the light of a serious suggestion. 'What good would water-gruel do them ?   And Government has something else to think about than knitting comforters for old men.   Ye might have thought of that.   But it isn't here as in heartsome Scotland, where a man doesn't speak unless he's got something to say.'

'I suppose,' asked Selwyn, 'that you are allowed a week or so to arrange all your affairs in Liverpool ?'

'Not me,' replied his friend vehemently ; 'those bloddy scoundrels—— Well, well, Mr. McClosky, saving your presence, it's just a word.   They've not given me more than two days, and how I'll get ready at all, devil a one of me knows.   There's my drawers and my desks here to be cleared out ; and they're every one chock full of the Lord knows what, that'll have to be sorted out.   And there's all my things to be packed, and lots of people to say good-bye to. I'll have to go now and begin. I'll see ye again to-night, Serle, you villain.'

'Stop a bit,' said Mr. McClosky. 'I'm a good deal older than you are, my lad, and I'm right glad you're promoted. But ye'll just take my advice, and hold yourself in hand. Ye're rash, and just a wee foolish. Now don't toss your head like that, for there's no sin like pride. Ye've got good brains, and a heart that's in the right place ; and ye'll may-be do well, though ye'd have a better chance if you wore the ribbon.'

'Phooh !' said Mr. Kerry.

'Well, if you won't it's a free country,' said Mr. McClosky, 'and no man's bound to be saved because a rope's thrown out to him. I'll only say this now : just try and get your head clear about tithes.'

'Tithes !' ejaculated Mr. Kerry, touched in his tenderest point. 'What is there about tithes that I don't know ?'

'A good lot, I'm thinking,' answered Mr. McClosky.

'I'd be glad to know it then,' Mr. Kerry

rejoined. 'Perhaps ye'll tell me. I haven't been learning for eight years to much purpose if I don't know it now.'

'Ah! Ye'll find out; have patience for a little while. Ye'll get into your troubles soon enough. Now be off and get your packing done, and come in here again before you go, just to shake hands.'

'A proud young man,' he soliloquized as the door closed behind Mr. Kerry; 'by pride the angels fell, and I doubt it'll be too much for poor Daniel Kerry.'

CHAPTER IV.

MR. KERRY'S FAREWELL.

IT was late on the same afternoon. Selwyn had worked hard all day at a task which was thoroughly uncongenial to him; and, in order that he might finish it, and half expecting Mr. Kerry to come in, he remained at his desk for nearly an hour after his chief and the clerks had gone. At length the last item was checked, and the balance taxable according to the Income Tax Acts duly brought out; the various accounts were separately tied up and endorsed with a statement of their contents; and then Selwyn got up from his chair, and, throwing both arms wearily over his head, wondered where Mr. Kerry could be, and why he had not kept his promise of coming in again that evening.

It was useless to stay there wondering, he decided, for Mr. Kerry's usual time of departure had long since passed, and it was now nearly seven o'clock. He changed his coat, therefore, and was just about to put on his hat, when the door opened. He turned round, thinking that Mr. Kerry must have returned for him, but it was Tom the porter who entered.

'What, Tom!' cried Selwyn, 'how is it you're not off duty? I thought you were only in charge in the daytime?'

'That's so, Mr. Serle; but I'm a bit late to-night. I wish you'd come upstairs, sir, into the laboratory—Mr. Kerry's there; and he's rather queer.'

'Queer? What do you mean?'

'Listen!' said Tom; 'you can hear him singing.'

He held the door open, and certainly Selwyn did hear a voice which, though muffled by the distance, he recognised as that of his friend, dolefully uplifted. He hastened up the narrow winding stairs which led from the corridor to the laboratory, followed closely by Tom, who explained :

' He do make such a noise, sir, when he's excited, that I thought I'd better come for you, for fear somebody else might hear him.'

On reaching the top of the stairs, Selwyn could at first see nothing, the gloom of the chamber, called by courtesy 'the laboratory,' seemed so profound. A single jet of gas at the farther side of the room revealed the darkness rather than dispelled it, and though there was also a lighted lantern, this had been placed on the ground behind a huge cask, so that it did not mend matters materially. The ceiling was vaulted, and had a damp, almost slimy appearance ; the walls were thickly ornamented with cobwebs, and the floor was strewn with fresh sawdust.

While Selwyn was taking in these details his eyes had adapted themselves to the want of light, and he was able to perceive the lank form of his friend seated astride on a cask. Mr. Kerry was apparently in the height of good spirits, for he was chanting lustily, while on the ground beside him sat his friend Tillotson of the Excise, in whose charge the laboratory had been left. Tillotson's face bore its gravest expression as he listened, with the greatest seriousness, to Mr. Kerry's song, beating gently on the sawdust with a pewter measure whenever any sentiment was expressed which bore upon love ; and, on the occasion of Mr. Kerry reaching a climax in his lay, Tillotson gathered himself together, and gave vent to a prolonged 'Hur-oo-oo-o!' which made the vaulted ceiling ring. But such interruptions were not well received by Mr. Kerry, who, on each occasion, paused, and cast a severe look downwards on the offender, ere gravely resuming his lay.

'See here, Tillotson,' said Mr. Kerry at last, 'if you can't stop bellowing in that way I'll have to put in a chorus, because there's a lot more verses yet, and you knock them all out of my head. Sure I've forgot already about the good priest being left on the roof in his shirt. Now, will you listen ? . . . . chorus, " Toory-oory-oory-oory, fol-de-liddle-oory." You may sing that after every verse. Now, leave me alone till I bid you open your mouth.' And the singer chanted :

> 'An' Judy said, "You're very kind,
>   I'll take a little taste,
> But not too much, nor yet too strong.
>   Here's luck !—but where's the praste ?"

Join in, man — chorus : " Toory-oory-oory-oory, fol-de-liddle-oory !" '

Tillotson's lungs found room for legitimate exercise in the chorus, which struck him as so beautiful, and so well adapted to the song, that he went on singing ' Oory-oory, fol-de-liddle,' long after Mr. Kerry had stopped and was looking at him with an air of intense astonishment.

' Oory-oory——' sang Tillotson.

' Will you hold your tongue ?' shouted Mr. Kerry, enforcing his question with a sharp rap with the pewter on his friend's head. ' You do it right enough, but you go on too long. Now listen again what Dan said—the thundering liar—when he knew all the time the poor praste was saying his prayers on the roof :

> ' And Dan replied, " He's safe inside
>   His own presbèeterce."
> " I didn't see him go," she said.
> " I did," said Dan McPhee.

Chorus :   " Toory-oory-oory-oory,   fol-de-
liddle-oory." '

A glance from Mr. Kerry warned Tillotson
against allowing his enthusiasm to run away
with him a second time ; and, rubbing his
head just where the new Surveyor's pewter
had fallen, he relapsed into silence, whilst
Mr. Kerry proceeded :

> ' " It's well he's not about," said Dan.
> " And that's the truth," said she,
> " There's whisky here enough for two—
> But not enough for three." '

It somehow happened this rather selfish
sentiment struck an answering chord in
Tillotson's breast.   He burst into the chorus
with an absolute howl of pleasure, and
screamed out ' Toory-oory, fol-de-liddle,
toory-oory-oory !' with a vehemence that
nothing could check.   He paid no attention
whatever to Mr. Kerry's remonstrances, and
only put up his hands to defend his head
from the assaults of the pewter measure.
Finally he sprang up from the floor, and,
tossing his arms into the air, began to execute
some wild kind of improvised hornpipe.   Mr.

Kerry several times adjured him to sit down and hear the rest of the song ; but to no purpose : he continued to dance more and more wildly, until, becoming giddy, he staggered up against Tom and Selwyn, who had been standing in the shadow of the entrance. He uttered a shrill scream of terror, not being aware of their presence ; and Tom, with an ejaculation of disgust, gave him a rough push, which caused Mr. Tillotson to measure his length on the floor. Mr. Kerry was as superstitious as he was high, and when he saw his friend's discomfiture, wrought by no visible means (for Selwyn and Tom were still standing in the shadow), he rose from the cask trembling all over, and called out :

'Holy St. Bridget bless and save us and keep us from a bad end ! What's there ? Come out of that and show yourself, if you're flesh and blood !'

'What else should I be ?' asked Selwyn, stepping forward ; 'have you lost your eyesight, Kerry ? You'd have seen me long ago, if you hadn't been so busy singing.'

'May I never drink again if it isn't that young snipe Selwyn, and Tom with him !'

exclaimed the Irishman, obviously relieved. He wiped his forehead of the sweat that had gathered on it, and then said : ' Sure, I knew you all the time, only I thought I'd frighten you a bit.'

'There was somebody frightened, right enough,' said Tom with a grin, and Selwyn answered :

'You're making a horrible noise up here, Kerry. Suppose we go and have some tea together. I haven't had mine yet.'

'More shame for you, then,' retorted Mr. Kerry, helping Tillotson up from the floor, and shaking him ; 'there, you're all right now. By the powers, he looks dazed ! Sit down, man, and you'll walk like a bishop by-and-by ;' with which remark he led the exciseman to a rough bit of staging placed against the wall, from which a cask had been removed, and propped him up with the utmost care. Then, as he stepped back with his head on one side to observe the effect of his work, he said scornfully, reverting to Selwyn's proposal : 'Tea is it that you'd have me drink ? I'm not going to do anything of the sort, then. I've tasted the blessed poteen this day, that's like the golden dew from heaven with the stars dissolved in it ; and it isn't likely I'm going to put any cat-lap down my throat after.'

With which remark he took up his pewter measure once more, and beating it against the cask on which he had been sitting, burst out :

' There, me boy, hear that tinkle ; like a harpstring with your fingers on it ! What's that now ? Tell me what it is that sings ?'

And, indeed, the cask did give forth the most musical note, quite as if some deep-toned instrument were really hidden in it.

' Whisky, I suppose,' said Selwyn.

' Faugh !' replied the Irishman ; ' it's the sweet air blowing, and the bees humming in the honeysuckle blossoms, and the cows coming home to milk, and the stream, with the trout in it, running under the alders, all singing together, my boy, and a lot more too, if you only knew it. Liquid gold, and sparkling sunlight, and life and strength to all creatures,' Mr. Kerry added, with a vague recollection of some scriptural phrase.

He sat down again on the cask as he finished speaking, and began singing in a half whisper : ' Toory-oory-oory, fol-de-liddle, toory-oory.' The very sound of these magic words produced an immediate effect on the motionless figure of Tillotson, propped up against the opposite wall. It stirred slightly, and ' Toory-oory ' was heard to issue from between its lips.

' Whurroo !' shouted Mr. Kerry, at the top of his voice ; ' the dead's come to life.'

' I say, Kerry, don't make such a noise,' entreated Selwyn ; ' some one will hear you.'

' Mr. Cramsey's come back, gentlemen,' observed Tom, who had disappeared for the last few minutes, 'and he's sitting working with his door ajar.'

' I don't care a twopenny damn for Mr. Cramsey or anybody else,' said Mr. Kerry ; and then, unconsciously quoting Marshal MacMahon, he added : ' I'm here, and I'm going to stay.'

Having made which statement, he burst out again into song :

> ' " But Danny, darlin'," Judy said,
>   " What's that upon the thatch ?"
> " It's cats, or rats, or bats," he said, . . .

I'm murdered if I've not forgotten the

last line ! But it doesn't matter, we'll take it out in chorus. Now, Tillotson, you divil, will you sing ? " Toory-oory, toory-oory !" '

Mr. Kerry bounced up and down on his cask, snapping his fingers above his head to give animation to the chorus, till he had wound himself up to the requisite pitch of excitement. Then, seizing Tillotson round the waist, he began to perform a kind of waltz, shrieking his chorus at the utmost power of his lungs. The noise reverberated from the roof, and echoed and re-echoed round the walls. Tom became infected with the burden of the chorus, and began to hum mournfully to himself :

' Toory-oory—we shall hear more of this ; fol-de-liddle—he's a regular demon when the drink is in him ; toory-oory—may I never, if Mr. Cramsey haven't got wind of him.'

At that moment the oily voice of Mr. Cramsey was indeed heard calling from the corridor below :

' Is hell broke loose up there ? It'll be bad for you if I have to come up to you.'

' Do be quiet, Kerry,' said Selwyn. ' You'll get into trouble.'

But Mr. Kerry paid not the smallest attention. He continued his dance, and shrieked, if possible, more loudly than before, till Mr. Cramsey lost patience, and his heavy step was heard on the stair. In an instant, as if he had been merely waiting for that, Mr. Kerry sprang to the gas-jet and turned it out. At thes ame moment he dashed the lantern on the floor, thus leaving the laboratory in total darkness, and, pushing Tillotson before him, and followed closely by Selwyn, he rushed down the stairs with such force as to propel Mr. Cramsey back into the corridor, and to throw him sprawling on his back. Before he could be identified by the astounded Surveyor he had turned out the gas in the corridor, and, with his two friends, made good his escape into the street.

' That's on account of old scores,' he observed, pausing to take breath at the bottom of Duke Street. ' Davey won't come to work in the evening again for a while, I'm thinking.'

He spoke quite soberly, and as if during his life he had never drunk anything stronger than water.

'Good-night, Tillotson,' he said. 'Serle, you're coming to my rooms ?'

And he thrust his arm through Selwyn's, and walked quietly up the street.

As they marched along Selwyn could not but marvel at the sudden change which had come over his companion. Whether the fresh air was the cause of it, or whether it was that Mr. Kerry's wild spirits had been only assumed, he could not decide. But certainly no one of the passers-by could have imagined that the sedate, grave man, who walked with a slight stoop, and listened to Selwyn's voice with an air of kindly interest, was the same with the whooping maniac who only ten minutes before had trundled Mr. Cramsey head over heels down the narrow laboratory stairs. Mr. Kerry's spirits had, in fact, taken a mournful turn.

' It's long it will be before we walk up here again together, Serle,' he observed. ' I'll think of Duke Street very often, and of Liverpool.'

' Perhaps you may be able to come back some day,' suggested Selwyn.

' And find everything changed ; all the old

houses pulled down and turned into shops, and Miss Dormer maybe married to some divil of a sea captain !'

'You can easily prevent that, you know,' answered Selwyn, 'if you choose.'

'And the old offices let to the Post Office as likely as not,' continued Mr. Kerry, wilfully disregarding his friend's insinuation, 'and all my old friends gone away or married, or dead, and Tillotson hung, maybe—'tis likely enough. No, Selwyn, don't you ever go back anywhere! It's no more like what it used to be than getting into your father's grave is like being with him when he was alive.'

With which cheerful remark Mr. Kerry, for almost the last time, put his latch-key into the door of Miss Dormer's house.

On the threshold of Mr. Kerry's sitting-room Miss Dormer met them. She was dressed in a nice brown dress, with thick folds of soft lace round her throat, and a silver brooch that her brother, who was drowned so many years ago (when she was quite a child, Miss Dormer used to say), had once brought her from Malta. The room was unusually neat, and decorated with flowers. The tea-table was adorned with a spotless cloth of the finest damask—damask that Miss Dormer only brought forth on the most solemn occasions. A cold tongue, garnished with salad, was flanked by a pair of fowls; and fancy bread of many shapes, with the freshest and coolest butter possible, all bore witness to the solicitude of Miss Dormer for her departing lodger. Something more there was in all this, Selwyn thought, than the ordinary care of a landlady; and if further evidence was wanted it might have been found by anyone who glanced at Miss Dormer's eyes, red and swollen, in spite of her cheerful looks. As she advanced to greet Selwyn she closed the door of Mr. Kerry's bedroom, which stood open, revealing a distinct prospect of trunks already packed.

'I can't bear to look at them,' she said, as if in order to explain her action.

'How very late you are,' she went on. 'I sat sewing in the window there, just where I could look all down the street, thinking every minute you'd be coming. Every time I heard a footfall I looked up, making sure it must be you. I grew quite nervous at last ; I began to think something must have happened.'

'Anxiety has done you good, Miss Dormer,' said Selwyn ; 'I never saw you look so well.'

Miss Dormer did indeed, despite her red eyes, look comparatively young, and almost pretty, as she stood in the window questioning Selwyn, and the last rays of sunlight tinged her hair with flame, and flashed . brightly from her glittering brooch. Even Mr. Kerry glanced at her with evident approval. Miss Dormer laughed at Selwyn's compliment, and simpered a little.

'But what *has* kept you ?' she asked.

'Business,' said Mr. Kerry oracularly ; but Selwyn answered :

'Kerry has been playing football with a Surveyor.'

'Mr. Cramsey !' gasped Miss Dormer, divining the truth. Then, clasping her hands together, she cried, 'He hasn't killed him ! Tell me, he hasn't hurt him !'

'No, no, Miss Dormer, don't be alarmed,' Selwyn answered. 'I don't think the man's hurt ; I only wish he were.'

'For shame!' interposed Miss Dormer, obviously relieved.

Then Selwyn went on to tell her how he had found Mr. Kerry in the laboratory, relating the scene with much humour, while from time to time Mr. Kerry, who sat regarding his friend with a grim smile, broke in with a correction, or an ejaculation, intended to elucidate the story.

As she listened Miss Dormer glanced once or twice at Mr. Kerry, as if some doubt crossed her mind, regarding which she needed to satisfy herself; but on each of these occasions she nodded reassuringly to herself. She frowned, however, when she heard how Mr. Cramsey had been cast downstairs, and she said to her lodger:

'You shouldn't be so violent, Mr. Kerry. You forget how strong you are. I'm afraid he'll have you up at the police court for this.'

'Phooh!' replied Mr. Kerry, snapping his fingers. 'How's he to know who it was? There wasn't as much light as a man could see to pick his teeth by.'

After which simile they sat down to tea;

and as the meal proceeded, and the twilight faded into dusk, and the dusk deepened into darkness, so that the lamp in the street shining in through the window threw a red gleam across the white tablecloth and the cups and saucers, Miss Dormer became very melancholy. She felt, in fact, as a condemned convict does when the day of his punishment is turning into night. She would fain have retarded the flight of the minutes, and hung a leaden weight on each. But they continued to fleet away, how fast! Surely never time went so quickly.

'I'll miss him sadly, Mr. Serle,' said she. 'I'll not know what the house is like without Mr. Kerry in it.'

'Of course you'll take another lodger,' said Mr. Kerry.

'Of course I shall do no such thing,' she retorted, a little vehemently. 'I don't need to take any at all, and that you know.'

There was a moment's pause, and from the sound of her voice (though it was too dark to see her face) Selwyn knew that she turned towards him.

'When Mr. Kerry is gone,' she said, ' I'll

keep the whole house to myself. It'll be very quiet, of course, and dull too. But it'll be better than having anybody else; and very likely some rackety man who'd want to have his friends here all night and sit screaming his songs when he ought to be in bed and asleep.'

Mr. Kerry was rather impressed by this devotion to his memory.

'Sure I'll write to you now and again,' he said, 'and tell you all I'm doing.'

Miss Dormer shook her head and sighed.

'Young men are so forgetful,' she said.

'And I'll come and see you, if you allow me,' said Selwyn.

'Will you, Mr. Serle? Will you really come? Now that would be kind. I should be so much pleased.'

'Selwyn won't be here long himself,' interposed Mr. Kerry, who did not quite relish the prospect of Miss Dormer enjoying long evenings *tête-à-tête* with a disengaged young man.

'Why, where's he going?'

'Oh, he'll be after getting transferred.'

Miss Dormer looked at Selwyn.

'It's one of Kerry's mad fancies,' Selwyn said. 'I have no intention at all of applying to be transferred,' added Selwyn a little sadly.

'It's that trolloping daughter of Trosdale's makes him say that,' ungallantly reflected Mr. Kerry, who did not know the London trip was to last indefinitely. 'Lord, if I hadn't spoken to Dandison, the lad would have been thicker than ever with Trosdale after I'm gone and there's no one to hold him back.'

The recollection of the wisdom he had shown in action brought a smile to Mr. Kerry's face, which was perceived by Selwyn, since Miss Dormer at that instant had lighted the gas.

'Well, I'm glad to hear it,' observed Miss Dormer; 'for to my mind young men are far too fond of wandering nowadays. They don't seem to know what the advantages of a quiet home are.'

'They would if they had once lived with you, Miss Dormer,' replied Selwyn. 'What are you laughing at, Kerry ?'

But Mr. Kerry stoutly maintained that he

was not laughing, although the last traces of his satisfied smile were still lingering round the corners of his mouth when Selwyn spoke.

They rose from table as the clock on the stairs struck ten.

'I ought to go,' said Selwyn. 'Shall I see you off in the morning, Kerry?'

'You might,' assented that gentleman, 'if you happen to be anywhere about Lime Street station at nine o'clock.'

'I'll arrange so that my affairs take me there. Good-night, Miss Dormer; it's not good-bye, you know, with me.'

But no cheerful words could assuage Miss Dormer's grief. She sighed audibly, and nearly shed tears as she took Selwyn's hand.

Mr. Kerry accompanied his friend to the door, and on returning to the sitting-room he found Miss Dormer with her head on the table shedding floods of tears.

CHAPTER V.

TRANSFERRED.

WHEN Mr. Kerry had taken his seat in the London train, and perceived that he had finally broken his connection with Liverpool, he was a proud and happy man. He felt no sort of regret at leaving that town. Although, during the six years which had sped by since he arrived in Liverpool, friendless and almost penniless, he had made many acquaintances among people who were congenial to him, his heart did not give one backward look as the train hasted through the green fields, unless it were towards Selwyn or Miss Dormer. For Selwyn, indeed, the Irishman entertained a sincere friendship, while Miss Dormer had ministered so assiduously to his physical comforts, and had been such an appreciative, submissive companion whenever he was alone, as to arouse in his heart a certain warmth of feeling for her.

These sentiments, however, were much too weak to interfere with the forward course of Mr. Kerry's thoughts. He felt like one who is freed from some long bondage. At a very early stage of his apprenticeship as Assistant-Surveyor he had conceived strong and clear ideas on the subject of his work, and had set himself vigorously about introducing them into his office. In this task he was continually thwarted by Mr. Cramsey, who threw an obstinate, unreasoning opposition in the way of all change, however clearly his Assistant might prove to him that it would be for the better. Kerry was not in those days the best tempered of men, and resented his chief's conduct so violently that for a long time there was almost open war in the office. Kerry, however, had enough intelligence to see that the Surveyor was too strong for him ; and he no sooner became thoroughly persuaded of this than he gave way with the best grace he could command. He did not by any means abandon his designs, and, in fact, managed to introduce most of them, by imperceptible degrees, in the course of years, but he chafed continuously under the restraint to which he was subjected, and longed for the day when he should be master of his own office, with no one to gainsay the methods by which he chose to do his work.

That time had now arrived—or he fancied it had; and his exultation in this thought was so great as to overmaster all other feelings. The opportunity had come to show his powers ; he would make it plain how far a man might go who possessed a clear head and an energetic will. 'Who knows,' reflected he, ' but in ten years I may be Chief-Inspector myself?' It was in this vein that he reasoned with himself all the way up to town, losing sight, like many a wiser man, of the realities of his position in the excitement of a sudden and long-hoped-for promotion.

Before he reached London he had per-suaded himself that the imperative wording of the letter from the Board which summoned him to town was inspired by some urgent necessity—some important duty must have turned up, he argued, which they wanted a trustworthy man to undertake. ' And, bedad, Danny !' he said, addressing himself in the affectionate tone which he reserved for occasions of perfect self-satisfaction, ' you'll have to pull yourself together now, my boy, and not disappoint them.'

Full of this idea, he entered the Chief-Inspector's room with the proud step and confident air of a man who believes he is about to receive some signal mark of distinction. He found it occupied, not, as he had expected, by Mr. Dandison, but by the Superintending-Inspector, Mr. Tenterden, a well-preserved middle-aged gentleman, whose ruddy features, pointed moustaches, and eye-glass practice were the envy of many younger civil servants.

' Ah, good-day, Mr. Kerry,' said this gentleman, when the messenger announced the name of the newly-appointed Surveyor ; ' we hardly expected you so soon. Pray sit down. I shall be at liberty in a few minutes.'

It was Mr. Tenterden's way to affect indifference to everything around him, especially to persons. He acted on some theory of his

own that all strangers were apt to take liber-
ties, and must, therefore, be carefully kept at
a distance. Few men liked Mr. Tenterden
until they had worked with him for some
years. They complained that they never got
within arm's length of him ; they often detected him scrutinizing them through his eye-
glass with what appeared to be supercilious
contempt, the expression of a man who has
much ado to refrain from bursting into a
shout of laughter, so absurd does he deem
something in his neighbour's manner or
appearance. Those, however, who were not
abashed by this behaviour, and especially
those who repaid his insolence in kind, woke
up some day to the fact that Mr. Tenterden
was to them a genial, kind-hearted friend,
always ready to do a service, just and
temperate towards his subordinates, firm and
independent towards his chiefs. It was a
thousand pities that it took so long to find
this out.

The Superintending-Inspector did not complete his letter without raising his eyes more
than once to regard Mr. Kerry with his
peculiarly stony stare. The new Surveyor

winced under this cold gaze : it was a thing
to which he was unaccustomed. Bluster or
insults he knew how to meet; but this sort of
reception quite disconcerted him.

'Well?' said Mr. Tenterden inquiringly,
when at last he had finished his letter. And,
as he uttered this exasperating monosyllable,
he turned half round in his chair, crossed his
legs, and fixed his eye-glass.

'May I die!' thought Mr. Kerry, 'if he
isn't looking at me as though I hadn't any
business here.'

'Well?' repeated Mr. Tenterden; and
finding that he received no answer, he added,
'and what do you think of doing with yourself now, Mr. Kerry?'

'Just whatever there is to do,' replied the
gentleman addressed.

'There isn't much,' his chief rejoined
doubtfully; 'a few books to index. Do you
like indexing, Mr. Kerry? If your handwriting is neat you might take a turn at that.'

Mr. Kerry sat absolutely aghast at this
suggestion, so fatal to his hopes of important
service. That he, after having mastered the
whole round of his duties, learning the Income

Tax Acts off by heart, and having at his fingers' ends every dodge and device necessary for dealing with the most crafty of fraudulent taxpayers—that he, recently appointed Surveyor, should be put to work at indexing, was a crushing blow.   There was also the inquiry whether his writing was good : that writing which he was wont to exhibit proudly as being 'more legible than print!'   These insults, heaped on him by a cool, nonchalant gentleman, who sat regarding him with a disdainful half smile, almost annihilated the unfortunate Irishman.

'We always had that done by the junior clerk in Liverpool,' he gasped at length.

'Ah, indeed!' said Mr. Tenterden carelessly.   'Well, after all, there *is* a writer here generally, and I don't know why you should do his work.'

There ensued a little pause.

'I really don't know what to suggest,' resumed Mr. Tenterden.   'Suppose you take a little walk, Mr. Kerry.   Or you might have a holiday for a few days ; run down and see your friends, you know.   Eh, what do you think ?'

'If there isn't anything for me to do here,' said Mr. Kerry in a tone of doleful disappointment.

'Not a mortal thing,' Mr. Tenterden assured him. 'The Secretary's away, too, and so is Mr. Dandison. You can sit here, if you like, you know, and see whatever is going on.'

'I'd like that best,' said Mr. Kerry.

'Very well. Then you may as well look in to-morrow about ten o'clock; and we'll see what we can find to do. Are you going now? well, *au revoir.*'

And before he had thoroughly realized that he was not in the least wanted at Somerset House, Mr. Kerry found himself in the Strand, with the rest of the afternoon on his hands. He did not know what to do with it. He had been recommended by Miss Dormer to stay at a boarding-house in the neighbourhood of Mecklenburgh Square, and had dropped his luggage there on the way to Somerset House. The dinner-hour was seven, so that he had still nearly four hours on his hands. He walked down to Waterloo Bridge, and stood gazing idly at the river for some time, till he was accosted by a ragged and dirty individual who wanted to borrow a shilling from him.

'Me wife and children's down with the fever,' he exclaimed ; but Mr. Kerry was not quite so inexperienced in the ways of cities as to be deceived by the first impudent rascal he met.

'I'll give you a penny,' he said ; 'that'll buy you bread and it won't buy drink. If it wasn't that you talk like an Irishman I'd not give you that.'

The beggar took the coin, and broke out into voluble cursings as Kerry walked away, more depressed than ever.

He spent the remainder of the day in wandering aimlessly about the streets ; and went to bed early, tasting to the full that peculiar wretchedness which is the doom of the busy man turned idle.

Next morning things were no better. He reached the office punctually at the time named by Mr. Tenterden ; but that gentleman had not yet arrived, nor did he make his appearance for nearly an hour. The interval was spent by Mr. Kerry in gazing out of window and in talking to the writer, who volunteered the information that work was 'slack just now;' to which Mr. Kerry replied by inquiring whether it was ever tight—a question which the writer did not seem able to answer satisfactorily, for he shrugged his shoulders, and asked if Mr. Kerry knew anything about horses. As the latter was pleased to appear indifferent on the subject, conversation flagged; and it was a relief to both when Mr. Tenterden entered.

'Hallo!' he said, in a tone of surprise, 'I thought you had gone on leave.'

'The last I heard was that I had best come here,' replied the Irishman sulkily; 'but it's my belief I might as well have stopped away.'

Mr. Tenterden fixed his eyeglass and turned his inscrutable gaze on the new addition to his staff.

'Well, we'll see what we can find for you to do,' he said.

He rummaged among his papers, and shortly brought forth the draft of a complicated return for the Treasury.

'This is completed, I believe,' he said,

handing the sheets to his subordinate; 'but you might look through the workings, and see if you notice anything wrong.'

Kerry seized it with avidity. It was not long before he pronounced it accurate, and drew his chief's attention to the fact that it had already been checked twice, by gentlemen whose initials were attached in guarantee of accuracy.

'Ah, so it has!' was the rejoinder. 'But it's impossible to be too careful with these things.'

Then, looking steadily at Mr. Kerry, the Superintending-Inspector said, as if stating something which must be new to his auditor: 'They're rather important, don't you know.'

This task was succeeded by another, and that by a third; but there were such long intervals between them that Kerry grew very impatient, and sorely weary. The day passed very slowly, and when, at its close, he rose up and took his hat, he felt more utterly jaded than at the end of the hardest day's work he had ever done in Second Liverpool.

More than a week passed in this way, and though Kerry became gradually habituated to spend a large part of every day in idleness,

he was by no means content. Mr. Tenterden
had promised that he should be sent to take
charge of the first district in which there was
a temporary vacancy, but at the end of a
month no such opening had occurred.

He received occasional letters from Selwyn,
from one of which he learned that the qualifying examination to which his friend was to
have submitted had been put off. Mr. Serle
was rather vexed at this, for, as he said, ' it
gave the other fellows time to pull up with
him.'

Selwyn's next communication announced
that Mr. Trosdale, having learned that Kerry
was in London, desired him to go to see
them if ever he had an evening to spare.
Mr. Kerry had a great many evenings on his
hands, and had he known that Mr. Trosdale
was in London, it is probable that he would
have called on him without an invitation.
That very evening, after dinner, he inquired
his way to Frith Street, and, after having
lost himself several times among the wind-
ings of Soho, he at last reached the dwelling
in which Mr. Trosdale had housed himself
and his daughter.

He found the ex-Surveyor in the most jovial of moods. He was delighted to see Kerry. When did he leave Liverpool? Why had he not come to see them before? He ought to have come to dinner, or at least to tea; but Madge should order tea again, since Kerry had dined late. And while it was being prepared they would take a turn round Soho Square, which was quiet enough at that hour, and enjoy a cigar. Did not Kerry like London? Pshaw, a young man of his age ought to be able to find a thousand amusements in town! Even he himself, though his sinews were relaxing, and his strength was not what it had been, found a glorious fulness about London, the satisfaction of many instincts which had mouldered in a provincial town. To be sure it was the dead season, but in a few weeks London would wake up again. Meantime, Kerry must come to Frith Street as often as he found time hanging heavily on his hands. Madge would be disengaged every evening, and he, unless by some accident, was never far away. Would Kerry come?

Of course Kerry would, and very gladly;

though he was sorely puzzled to understand this outbreak of geniality on the part of the ex-Surveyor. He expressed his thanks, and followed his host into the house, still wondering what it could mean. Madge was presiding over the tea-tray, and at once plied him with questions about Liverpool, being obviously much disappointed at finding he had left that town very shortly after her own departure. However, if Mr. Kerry could tell her little about Liverpool and Selwyn, he had much to say about his own proceedings since his arrival in London ; and he described his occupations in Somerset House, as well as the personality of Mr. Tenterden, with a drollery which made both his hearers laugh heartily. Then he diverged into stories of his early life in Ireland, which he told with much native humour, and a frank simplicity which delighted Madge.

The visit was certainly a successful one. Mr. Kerry parted with his host on the best of terms, and received a hearty invitation to repeat his visit.

Madge felt, in truth, exceedingly dull. The life they led was very well for her father, as he enjoyed the excitement of interviews with persons of many kinds, who could, if they pleased, assist him in the matter of the furnace. He was generally out the whole day, and, until his return, Madge's time, was at her own disposal. For a few weeks she enjoyed visiting the different places of interest, and passed many pleasant hours in the National Gallery. The afternoon service in the Abbey was a great pleasure to her. The thought that every conceivable kind of trouble must, within the centuries, have been lightened within those walls, made it seem easier for her there to lay down a part of her own burden. And the relief was sorely needed, for she began to surmise that her father had no intention of returning to Liverpool, and though she strove to think bravely of the future, she saw no security in it.

From these melancholy thoughts the visits of Mr. Kerry proved an agreeable diversion. The Irishman was always talkative and amusing; he had become more quiet, too, since the change in his position, more subdued, and less confident of his own superiority. Madge thought him decidedly a pleasant companion, in spite of his uncultured manners, and she was herself surprised at perceiving with what pleasure she at last looked forward to his visits, and how insipid the days seemed on which he did not come.

She was on the point of writing to Selwyn to tell him how much the Irishman was brightening her life, when she received a letter from Liverpool, written in great haste, to announce that instructions had arrived from London for Mr. Serle to proceed to Reading to work under the Surveyor in that town. The letter was full of eagerness and pleasure at the prospect of being within such distance of his friends as to make it possible for them to meet occasionally. He begged for instructions in whose charge he should leave the house; and Mr. Trosdale, on being consulted on this point, at once made up his mind to terminate his tenancy, and to sell such of the furniture as he could not deposit in the narrow space of their lodgings. He paid no attention to Madge's suggestion that the furniture might be stored until they could form some definite plan for the future, but wrote that day to a house-agent, in whose hands he placed all the arrangements. He was good enough to express satisfaction at the prospect of having Selwyn once more within reach, and added that 'it would be a convenience, because the young fellow doesn't know how to explain himself in a letter.' This was a charge to which Selwyn could not retort, because Mr. Trosdale had very seldom, during all the weeks of their separation, vouchsafed to write to him ; and then only a few lines at a time, full of grumbling at the inconvenience of letters.

Mr. Kerry's satisfaction was not equal to that of the Trosdales when he heard of Selwyn's removal. He was quite ignorant of the existence of any engagement between Madge and Selwyn, for the ex-Surveyor had either forgotten such an unimportant matter, or for some reason of his own had decided not to allude to it. Kerry thought himself quite at liberty to make what efforts he could to engage Madge's affections ; and as he could not fail to perceive that she enjoyed his visits, he was beginning to feel very sanguine about the result. His hopes were, however, nipped by an untimely frost ; for, on the next morning, when he reached Somerset House, he found Mr. Tenterden reading a telegram, which that gentleman immediately placed in his hands. It ran as follows:

' *From*	' *To*
MRS. TOOMER, Carlisle.	The CHIEF INSPECTOR OF TAXES, Somerset House, London.

' Mr. Toomer seized with gastric fever. Likely to be ill some weeks.'

' Now, then, Mr. Kerry,' said the Chief-Inspector, 'take a hansom back to your lodgings; pick up your bag, and be off by the first train you can catch. You must be in Carlisle to-night!'

Kerry had only time to write a short note to Mr. Trosdale announcing his departure, and, long before it reached Frith Street, he was in the train speeding northwards.

What Selwyn thought of Reading is not material to the purposes of this story, for, on the second morning after his arrival in that town, he received an intimation that the Board had seen fit to transfer him again to a fresh district, and, to his surprise and delight, he found he was to be sent to the Metropolis. Of Stratford, the district selected, Selwyn had hardly heard before; and he did not greatly concern himself as to its precise situation. It sufficed for him to know that it must be within easy reach of Frith Street. He never doubted that he should be able to live with the Trosdales as before; and it was a keen disappointment, therefore, to learn, on reporting himself at Somerset House two days later, that he would be expected to reside in his district.

'How else can you know it properly?' asked Mr. Tenterden, who had taken up Mr. Dandison's duties for the time; 'it is imperative, Mr. Serle, that you should live at Stratford. You might come as far west as Bow, perhaps, but certainly no further.'

With his spirits considerably dashed, Selwyn plodded eastwards, and put himself, according to instructions, on the top of a tram which started from Aldgate, and which, after a ride of three-quarters of an hour through streets which were not attractive, deposited him in the Broadway, Stratford, feeling perfectly indifferent about the reception he might meet with.

He found the Inland Revenue Office without difficulty. It was in the possession of a tall, thin young lad, with a red face and close-cropped fiery hair, who answered Selwyn's inquiry for Mr. Carthew by assuring him, in a rich brogue, that the Surveyor had gone home, and added, on his own account, the information that he generally did so about three o'clock.

'And it's now nigh upon four,' he continued; 'so, if you want to see him, you'll have to wait till to-morrow.'

'Does he live far from here?'

'What would I be telling you that for?' asked the clerk suspiciously. 'Is it a writ you're going to serve on him?'

Selwyn laughed outright.

'Do I look like a process-server?' he asked. 'No, it's only a letter I wish to deliver personally.'

'Give it me,' said the clerk, stretching out his hand. 'Well, tell me what's in it, then, and I'll be able to advise you.'

'I don't want any advice, thank you,' replied Selwyn; 'I only wish for Mr. Carthew's address. My letter is from Somerset House, and I must deliver it myself.'

The answer which the red-headed clerk was about to make was interrupted by a loud shouting in the street.

' It's himself again, or I'm a lost sinner !' exclaimed the lad delightedly, and running to the window, he threw it up.

Selwyn followed him with some curiosity to learn who 'himself' might be, and why his movements should cause such interest in the Tax Office. He saw an elderly man of slight figure slouching along the pavement, followed by a crowd of children and a few grown women, who were pressing round him, apparently urging him to do something which he steadily declined to attempt. Their importunities, however, became at last so pressing that he turned so as to face his tormentors, and, with a muscular sweep of his arm, which struck two or three children backwards, cleared an open space around him, and addressed the crowd in an angry tone :

' Aren't ye ashamed, ye dirty, ignorant blackguards, that haven't any more manners than if you'd never seen a gentleman ! Can't you let me be, ye gutter-raking, misbegotten little devils ? Do you think I've no other business than to pleasure you ?　Be off, now, or I'll have a poleeshman on the backs of everyone of ye.'

This exhortation produced nothing more than a shout of laughter and derision.

'Pipe up!' cried the boys ; 'tip us a song. We won't go away unless you do.'

'Won't ye, ye onreasonable little imps, won't ye go away ?　We'll see about that. I'll teach you to disgrace a gentleman under the windows of his own office !'

He made a dart at the urchin nearest him, but the lad was too quick, and dodged out of his reach, and after one or two other efforts to scatter the throng, finding it impossible, he resigned himself to the inevitable.

'Be quiet, then,' he said, holding up his hand ; ' I'll sing you a song, since you must have it.　It's about a relation of mine.　His sister was Molly Burke, of Fermanagh, and she married my grandmother's uncle.　Bedad, it's a sweet ballad !'

'Who is this remarkable individual ?' asked Selwyn.

'It's me uncle,' said the clerk proudly. 'He's the best ballad-singer on this side of

the Channel ; and on the other there's only
Tim Rooney, of Comber, can touch him.'

Meantime the gentleman in the street had
begun, in a not unmusical voice, the following
ballad :

> 'The *Nancy Bell* she went to h—ll
>   In seventeen forty-four ;
> Brave Captain Burke commanded her,
>   And twice a hundred more.

> 'Says Burke, says he, "I never see
>   The Frenchman that could fight ;
> We'll have them all, both great and small,
>   Before another night."

> 'So up he slips between the ships,
>   And blazes right and left, ...'

'Now then, move on—move on, please !'
said a rough voice, as a burly policeman came
scattering the crowd of enthralled listeners
right and left. 'Move on, please ; we can't
have you stopping up the way. Move on,
come now !'

In a trice the urchins had disappeared, and
the ballad-singer was left confronting the
constable.

'I wish,' remarked the former, 'I had you
on the banks of the Liffey ; I'd teach you to
interfere with a gentleman's amusement.'

And he walked off; while the officer, having no retort ready, proceeded on his beat.

‘ Here he comes,’ said the proud nephew, as footsteps were heard ascending the stairs.

‘ What is he coming up here for ?’ asked the astonished Selwyn.

‘ Because it’s his office, to be sure !’ and, in another moment, the ballad-singer was in the room.

‘ Here’s a gentleman with a letter for Mr. Carthew,’ explained the red-headed clerk; ‘and, faith ! it must be mighty important, because he won’t let me see the inside of it.’

Mr. Murphy drew himself to the extreme height which his stature permitted, and eyed Selwyn from head to foot with a supercilious gaze.

‘ Were you a witness, sor, of that disgraceful scene ?’ he inquired.

‘ That’s a hard name to give it,’ said Selwyn. ‘ I heard part of a ballad sung in a very taking style.’

‘ It was disgraceful, sir ; it is abominable, I say, that a gentleman can’t be fond of the ancient practice of ballad-singing, and indulge himself just occasionally in the Broadway here on Saturday nights in an old hat and coat, without being recognised whenever he goes out, and followed by a pack of onmannerly devil's brats like them you saw. It's my one pleasure, sorr; it's the only relic of happier days, when I was respected and looked up to in me native country, when I'd have cracked the skull of any man who dared to hint I should some day hire myself out to scribble at the bidding of an English Surveyor of Taxes.'

It would be difficult to convey an idea of the scorn which Mr. Murphy threw into the last words of this speech. His eyes flashed, and he terminated with an emphatic gesture which seemed to show that already, in imagination, he beheld the Saxon Surveyor prostrate before him, and refrained only out of generosity from dancing on his body.

'So you are a clerk in this district?' said Selwyn.

'I am very much at your service,' rejoined the clerk, with a low bow; 'and if you want Mr. Carthew, I shall be happy to act as his substitute.'

But this obliging offer Selwyn declined, and, having obtained the Surveyor's address, he bade good-day to the clerks, and set out to deliver his letter personally, greatly exercised in his mind at finding precisely the same order of clerks he had known in Liverpool wasting their sweetness in the great Metropolis.

'My mind misgives me, Terence,' said Murphy, when he had gone. ''Tis a proud, hard-fisted fellow. Why wouldn't he show me the letter? Sorrow light on him, is it me that he shows his slight to?—me, Phil Murphy! Bedad, I was too civil to him!'

'What do you think his letter is about?'

''Tis that makes me onaisy, me boy. 'Tis that way they send down Assistant-Surveyors; and I misdoubt he's one.'

'If so, they'll be getting rid of us,' suggested Terence.

'They'll maybe want one to go,' replied his uncle; 'but I'll not see ye wronged, Terence. Ye're me own sister's son, and it was never said of Phil Murphy that he forgot his flesh and blood. So now shut up shop, and we'll go over to the Sceptre; for it's a glee night, and we may as well be early.'

Mr. Carthew lodged in a little house in the Bow Road, set back somewhat further from the highway than those adjoining it, and having consequently a longer garden in the front. As Selwyn opened the gate, on which 'Linden Villa' was painted in letters which had once been white, a tall figure rose from a stooping posture beside a bed of carnations which were in full flower, and stood erect looking at Selwyn as he advanced up the path.

'Do you want me ?' asked Mr. Carthew, in answer to Selwyn's inquiring look. 'What can I do for you ? Will you not walk in if you wish to speak to me ? Here it is too noisy to talk.'

Selwyn followed Mr. Carthew into a small room opening from the hall, which was fitted up as a kind of study, and handed to him Mr. Tenterden's letter. As he read it, Selwyn had time to notice that his new chief stooped almost as much as if he was slightly deformed. His forehead was high, but the lines of his face were loose, and bore witness to a certain weakness of character which Selwyn had already detected, or so he thought, from the manner of Mr. Carthew's speech.

' This is quite a surprise to me,' said the Surveyor of the Stratford district. ' I had no intimation from the Board that I was to expect you, Mr. Serle.'

' Indeed ; that is rather surprising.'

' Yes ; very unusual. I don't know what to make of it. Do you think there is any mistake ?'

' That would seem to me more extraordinary still. Is it possible that the letter to you can have been overlooked ?'

' Quite possible, I'm afraid. My clerk, Murphy——'

He broke off suddenly, with a vexed expression in his face.

' The gentleman with a turn for ballad-singing ?' observed Selwyn.

' How did you know that ? Have you been to the office ?'

' It was there I obtained your address, and heard the gentleman's recital,' Selwyn returned.

' I wish I could get rid of that fellow. The Inspector will see him some day. Tell me what he was doing.'

Thus appealed to, Selwyn described the

absurd scene he had witnessed. He was many times interrupted by expressions of annoyance from the Surveyor ; and when he related how Murphy had actually favoured the crowd of his admirers with a ballad beneath the very windows of the Tax-Office, Mr. Carthew's vexation reached its climax.

'I declare,' he said, 'this is intolerable! I must do something with the fellow. I can't stand his ways any longer. I shall tell him to-morrow that he must go.'

Selwyn made no remark ; if he had broken silence, it would have been to state his opinion that this step might well have been taken long before. Some thought of this kind was probably passing through Mr. Carthew's mind, but he checked himself as he was about to speak again, and stood silent for some minutes, drumming incessantly on the mantelpiece with his finger.

'If you will excuse me,' Selwyn said at last, 'I think I must leave you, for I have not yet found lodgings.'

'My landlady has two rooms to let. Why should you not take them ? I can recommend her : she is clean and civil, and, if you will allow me to say so, I think it would be pleasant for me to have some companionship out of office hours. I have not many friends, Mr. Serle; one has not many, you know, when one passes middle life.'

'You are very kind,' said Selwyn; and indeed he felt that the Surveyor's suggestion was considerately made.

He said as much, and Mr. Carthew seemed pleased, and rang for his landlady.

The bargain was soon struck: the rooms were clean and comfortable, and the landlady not more grasping than others of her calling. Selwyn was disposed to think that he had fallen into good hands, and having declined a pressing invitation to stay and dine with his new chief, he set out for Frith Street, his heart beating with the pleasurable anticipation of taking his friends by surprise.

A surprise it was; but beyond all doubt a joyful one.

The Surveyor laid aside his paper, and condescended to be genial. He produced a bottle of champagne, and drank the health of the Assistant-Surveyor newly appointed to Stratford, and confusion to the curmudgeon of an Inspector who insisted on his living in that God-forsaken district.

'It wasn't so when I entered the service,' he lamented plaintively ; 'there were none of these silly restrictions then. We all worked cordially together; and if a Surveyor wanted a day's shooting, or had to go to the other end of the country on business, he just dropped a line to his Inspector unofficially, and the thing was winked at. Why, I remember Phillips, of Barnstaple, applying for three months' leave on the ground that his constitution " wanted tone." And by George, sir, he got it !'

Then he made Selwyn tell him in detail all he had been doing since they parted ; and Madge sat opposite to them listening with such tender interest, and interposing from time to time so sweetly, that Selwyn felt his happiness was ' too great almost to last.' It could not last long, indeed ; for Frith Street, Soho, and Stratford lie far apart; and best part of the evening was over before he reached the Trosdales' lodgings. He rose unwillingly when the clock struck ten, and went out into the sweet night air with many thoughts. and fancies in his brain wholly new and strange to their habitation, which furnished him with matter for happy musing long after he had reached his lodging, and in fact after he should have been asleep.

He was aroused the next morning by an intimation that Mr. Carthew was waiting breakfast for him. It was already nine o'clock, and he dressed hastily, and descended with a feeling of shame at having overslept himself. The Surveyor was sitting beside the window, opening and reading his official correspondence.

' Good-morning, Mr. Serle,' he said. ' I was sorry to disturb you. You see, I have been up to the office already, and found the letter announcing your arrival. It came yesterday, I suppose, and I don't know why it wasn't given to me. However, let us have breakfast now.'

' I am sorry to be so late,' said Selwyn ; ' and sorry also that you waited breakfast for me.'

' I did not expect you would appear very early,' replied his chief. ' As for me, I am generally up at six. But that is the kind of habit which creeps upon one only when one begins to realize how little time there is in life for anything but unpleasant duties.'

Then he handed over to Selwyn half a dozen letters.

'If you can read as you eat,' he said, 'you may as well look through these. You will get an idea from them of the position of our work.'

'It seems to be in a fairly forward state,' Selwyn said, after reading the letters carefully. 'I wish you would tell me more about your clerks before we go to the office; I should like to know whether they are to be trusted.'

'The young man, Adair, is a nonentity. He works steadily enough under his uncle's eye; but if Murphy won't work himself, as often happens, not a stroke can anyone get out of the nephew. Then as for Murphy— well, you saw him. He's not very intelligent, but he knows the work from beginning to end, and does it when he feels inclined. He's as vain as a peacock, not too truthful, and impatient of the slightest word of reproof. That's his official character. Out of the office he loves nothing so much as singing ballads; he

belongs to every glee club east of Aldgate,
and, as you know, he is not content with airing
his cracked voice at tavern concerts, but goes
out sometimes into the very streets.'

'Not an attractive picture,' said Selwyn;
'is he the best clerk you can find?'

'Oh, I beg your pardon. I find Murphy
most attractive. Just compare him with the
average Surveyor's clerk, the dull, plodding
booby that haunts, I dare say, half the Tax-
Offices you know, or the dissipated blackguard
who is sodden from morning till night with
beer. Murphy is never drunk in the daytime;
and when you come to know him better you'll
be inexpressibly grateful to him for the drollery
of his sayings. He gives quite a picturesque-
ness to our routine life.'

'You seem to feel the monotony keenly.'

'I do,' the Surveyor replied with emphasis;
and again Selwyn could not but be struck by
the mental likeness between Mr. Carthew and
Mr. Trosdale, as he had been amazed to find
Thistlethwaite's double in Murphy. 'With
me it is always pulling against the collar.
And then there is such frightful waste of time.
If I might close my office doors I could finish

my work in about five hours a day. But from morning till night I am annoyed with visitors. Six out of seven want nothing, the seventh doesn't know what he wants ; and so among them they cut off a fearfully large amount of my precious leisure.'

Then, seeing Selwyn glance towards the book-shelves, he added :

' Yes, those are my friends, whose voices I hear calling me to return all the day long. But if you have finished, let us go up to the office.'

Meanwhile Mr. Phil Murphy and his nephew had already arrived there.

' Tol-de-roll, tara-diddle-rum,' sang Murphy n his high-pitched voice ; ' this'll be a day of battles, Terence, I'm thinking. Hold your head up, and show your spirit in the face of the foe.'

' Me head aches,' said the red-headed boy mournfully ; ' sure I told you Mowlem's whisky was too strong.'

' Divil a twist it's given me,' said his uncle jauntily. ' Go and hold your head under the tap ; 'twill be as steady as a rock by the time Carthew comes.' And as the young man departed on this errand, Murphy burst into full song :

> ' "Oh, Mary darlin', 'twas your eye
> That beamed on me so sweetly ;
> Those lips so red, that winning smile,
> That broke my heart completely."

That's a sweet song, Phil Murphy ; my own father's cousin made it when he lived in Enniskillen, and nearly died because a silly slip that was there wouldn't have him ; more by reason——'

He stopped short and drew himself up to his full height here, for he perceived that Mr. Carthew and Selwyn had just entered the office.

'Good-morning, Mr. Murphy,' said the Surveyor ; 'this is Mr. Serle, who is to be the Assistant in the district.'

Murphy executed the stiffest of bows.

' I saw the gentleman yesterday,' he observed.

'Oh, then there's no introduction needed.' And the Surveyor passed on with Selwyn into the inner room.

Immediately afterwards the outer door

opened to admit Terence Adair, and with him the most dismal boo-hooing that could be imagined.

'Be easy, my boy—be easy, I tell you!' cried his uncle; but Terence persisted in howling and blubbering, not suspecting that his chief had arrived.

'What on earth is all this about?' asked Mr. Carthew, coming to the door of his room; and once again Selwyn was forcibly reminded of his experiences in Third Liverpool.

'It's me head!' sobbed Terence; and 'It's his head, sorr,' said Murphy. 'He was reading Acts of Parliament all night with a towel dripping on the book; and ye see how it's ended,' he added reproachfully.

'Do be reasonable, Murphy,' remonstrated the Surveyor. 'I didn't ask him to sit up all night, or even to read any Acts at all. If he'd do his work in the daytime I should be quite content. But if there's anything the matter with his head, for Heaven's sake send him home! We can't have that noise here.'

'Run round to Mowlem, Terence darlin','

said his uncle, when the Surveyor had gone, 'and make him give you a cup of strong coffee. Strong, mind you! and just walk about a bit, and don't come back again.'

And having packed off his precious nephew, Murphy set about examining a bundle of Revenue tax returns, humming as he did so—

> ' A hundred ships, a thousand men,
> A thousand rifles laid in store,
> The old brave spirit back again,
> And Ireland is our own once more.'

CHAPTER VI.

'I THINK,' said Mr. Carthew, some half-hour later, standing before the chimney-piece in the outer office, 'that you had better sit out here, Mr. Selwyn. Then you can see the people who call; and if you could settle everyone of the cases, I should be infinitely obliged to you.'

'And where's the lad Terence to sit?' inquired Murphy, with a look of defiance which was in itself a gage of battle.

'I do not know,' replied the Surveyor, weakly declining the challenge. 'I haven't settled that. Wait till he comes to-morrow.'

Lest anything further should be said, Mr. Carthew at once went back to his inner office, requesting that he might not be disturbed, as he was anxious to complete an additional assessment that day.

Selwyn took possession of the chair assigned to him, and of the correspondence which his chief had handed over. He ventured on one or two remarks to Murphy, elicited by the nature of his work, but met with such curt and abrupt replies that he relapsed into silence.

As he pursued his occupation, however, he was aware that the clerk was darting furious glances at him, contorting his face when he thought Selwyn did not see him, and doing his best to concentrate into a look the scorn and contempt he felt for all interlopers, and for Selwyn in particular. He appeared to be doing his best to lash himself into a state of fury : now he tapped on the table nervously with his pencil ; now he gasped as if he were about to burst forth into a torrent of abuse ; and more than once he got up and walked across the office without any apparent cause. At last he sprang from his seat and went into Mr. Carthew's room, where Selwyn heard his voice raised in angry controversy for perhaps

a quarter of an hour.   At the end of that time
he came back looking flushed and indignant,
and having carefully shut the door of communication between the two rooms, he began
in a rich and oily brogue :

'In Oireland, sorr, we've got different
notions from what ye have in this counthry.'

'Indeed,' said Selwyn, laying down his
pen.   'Pray explain yourself more fully.'

'I'm your humble servant, sorr,' rejoined
the Irishman, making use of the phrase with
which he habitually expressed acquiescence
with a tinge of contempt in it.   'In me own
counthry, we're more sensitive ; and we've
got keener ideas of honour than ye have
here.   We don't submit tamely to an insult,
sorr ; we resent it, and if it's necessary we
wipe it out, sorr.'

'Really, Mr. Murphy,' answered Selwyn,
'I do not in the least understand you.   I
may say, however, I have no wish to interfere with your avenging any insult you may
have received in the way you think proper.'

'Faith,' said Murphy gleefully, 'I begin
to think you're a gentleman of honour after
all.   I'll tell you how it stands, sorr.   You've

put an affront on me, and on me nephew
Terence, by intruding yourself in this district,
and still more by not going out of it when
you found you were doing injury to my
prospects, and my nephew's prospects.'

'Well, Mr. Murphy,' rejoined Selwyn,
hardly able to avoid smiling at the fantastic
dignity of the tall, spare figure before him,
' I am sorry for that. But I don't see how
it can be helped.'

'Ye don't ! There's only one way of
settling differences between two men of
honour.'

' Do you mean to say,' asked Selwyn, 'that
you are inviting me to have a shot at you ?'

' Just that,' answered the Irishman ; and
so saying, he quickly opened the drawer of
his desk and brought out a mahogany case.
'See there,' he said proudly, 'there's the
pistols me own uncle shot Sir Tim Rooney
with on a bit of a field behind Limerick.
Crosshandles they are, and a pair of lovely
tools.'

He balanced them affectionately in either
hand, then looked closely at the stock of one
of them.

'T. R., 1817,' he read with some difficulty. 'That's Sir Tim.   Many's the time I've heard my uncle tell about that day ; more by reason that he was a bit downhearted, for he wasn't sure his hand was steady.   We'll have to do without friends, I'm afraid, and that's not right.   But maybe you could find two safe men who wouldn't mind meddlin' in a little affair of this kind ?   Well, if not, it's a pity ; but we'll do without them.'

Then he sprang up and laid down his pistols.

'I was forgettin',' he said.   'It's so long since I've had an affair of the kind.   I must put the affront on you.'   And without more to do he struck Selwyn a stinging blow on the face with his open hand ; whereupon the latter, though he had been far from expecting any such development of the conversation, skilfully knocked Mr. Murphy down.

The Irishman fell backwards over a chair, striking his head heavily against the fender. His fall upset several weighty assessments, and the crash immediately brought out the Surveyor.

'Good heavens !' exclaimed Mr. Carthew,

seeing his senior clerk lying motionless, with a thin stream of blood trickling across his collar from the gash made by the corner of the fender, 'what on earth has happened ? Is he drunk, Mr. Serle ?'

'I don't think so,' replied Selwyn, stooping over his fallen adversary. 'Kindly give me the caraffe, Mr. Carthew. He'll be all right presently.'

He bathed Murphy's temples with cold water, and in a very few minutes that gentleman opened his eyes and turned them reproachfully on Selwyn.

'You shouldn't have struck so hard,' he said, rather faintly ; and with that he sat up, and then rose to his feet, and stood supporting himself by the mantelpiece, looking very pale and ghastly.

'I believe the man's seriously hurt,' said the Surveyor, in some alarm. 'Did you do this, Mr. Serle ? What could have been your object ?'

'It's all right, sorr,' said Murphy. 'I put the affront on him. It's just a matter between ourselves ; only he might have proportioned his blow.'

' I won't undertake to do anything of the kind, Mr. Murphy,' replied Selwyn, still somewhat heated; 'that's another point, I suppose, in which the English practice diverges from yours ?'

' Faith, I believe it is !' rejoined Murphy, putting his hand to his head.

' I wish one of you would tell me what this is all about,' said the Surveyor irritably. ' You seem to consider I'm the last person who ought to ask any questions, no matter what disturbance may be made in my office.'

' I do not think that, Mr. Carthew,' said Selwyn ; ' but I really consider this little accident is not worth inquiring into.   I should be obliged if you would let it pass.   It is not likely to be repeated.'

' I'm sure I hope not.   Well, if you won't tell me, I'll go back to my work.   But do keep the office quiet, Mr. Serle ; it's by the merest good luck some one of the public has not come in in the midst of this.'

Then, going up to Murphy, he surveyed him from head to foot.

' Had not you better go home ?' he asked. ' You look very groggy.'

'I think I will,' said Murphy. 'I'm not so young as I was by a good bit. Time was when I'd have been none the worse for a trifling accident like this. I fell from top to bottom of the stairs of my uncle's house in Mountjoy Square, the night he entertained the Chief Baron, and we all went out into the streets with sticks after dinner, and laid about us. But I'm not the good man I was. Good-day to ye, Mr. Serle.' And turning back, as his hand was on the lock, he whispered, 'Ye'll hear from me this afternoon, or maybe to-morrow morning.'

It was only as he watched him leaving the room that Selwyn observed he moved very feebly, and had a certain appearance of age about him which was not noticeable whilst he was speaking and acting under excitement. Selwyn felt great compunction for having struck a man so much older than himself; and sat down again to his work with an uneasy feeling that he had begun badly in his new district.

The rest of the day passed quietly. Neither of the clerks returned, and it so happened that during the whole afternoon the public abstained from visiting the office. Great pro-

gress was therefore made by both the Surveyor and his Assistant; and when, about
half-past four, Mr. Carthew emerged from his
sanctum, and suggested that they should close
the office, he appeared highly content with
himself.

'I don't know when I've had such a quiet
time,' he said with a yawn. 'Do you think
we could get on without any clerks at all,
Mr. Serle?'

'Do you suppose it's likely to come to that?
The office would be much quieter, certainly.'

'I don't know what it will come to, I'm
sure. There was Murphy telling me this
morning that if I turned away that useless
nephew of his he'd go too.'

'I should not have thought family affection
was so strongly developed in Murphy.'

'Ah! you don't know him yet. It isn't
so much family affection, as affection for
his family, if you understand my distinction.
I mean that I don't think Murphy has the
least regard for his nephew personally; but
he thinks a slight put on any member of his
family recoils more or less on himself, and
resents it accordingly.'

'He is a strange fellow.'

'He's a very useful one,' rejoined the Surveyor, yawning again. 'I hope he won't go; but if he will, he must. As for Adair, I shall be heartily glad to see the last of him.'

As soon as the office was closed, Selwyn made his way to Frith Street, where he was received with the same kindness as on the previous day. They had waited tea for him, and when it was over Mr. Trosdale carried off Selwyn into an upper room which was consecrated to the mysteries of the furnace. There, upon a low bench, stood three models, which made a goodly show; but with the exception of two rickety chairs there was no other furniture in the room.

'We have not made much progress,' the ex-Surveyor began, as soon as he had closed the door behind his young friend.

'I am sorry to hear that,' replied Selwyn; 'what has happened?'

'Why nothing, that's the whole difficulty. Everybody speaks favourably of the furnace— they all like that well enough; but somehow nobody takes it up. Hodson had just paid a large sum, so he said, for an improvement, and did not feel inclined to dip further into his pocket. The pettifogging fellow! I told him having wasted a few thousands on a worthless idea was no reason for sending me away.'

'Then there was Clutterbuck,' said Selwyn ; 'did you call on him ?'

'I called on everybody. Clutterbuck's partner would not hear of dealing with me, wanted to economize, didn't want to make larger profits, liked a safe business—didn't like brains, in fact, and cared for nothing but stupidity. Heaven grant me patience ! I sometimes go very near to losing it.'

'And Johnstone, what of him ?'

'At first he seemed the most reasonable of them all, quite disposed to do business. But somehow he cooled off, and wouldn't even give me a reason for declining.'

'How terribly disappointing !' exclaimed Selwyn.

'Isn't it ? Here are three months of precious time gone without gaining one step. I'm not disheartened, though ; I always knew there would be this sort of thing at first.'

Selwyn could not help reflecting that if

this were true Mr. Trosdale had been especially careful not to disclose his anxieties. But he kept silence, and the Surveyor went on :

'You don't know much of the histories of great inventions ; but I can tell you that my experience has been that of everybody who has succeeded eventually. I should have been low-spirited and anxious now if I had not met with these rebuffs.'

'I'm glad to find you still so confident,' said Selwyn ; 'after all, a good heart is half the battle.'

'Of course, you see, I know the value of the furnace ; nothing could make me doubt that. So I have the less cause for depression. Now here are a lot of letters from persons I am going to call on next week. You might as well look through them.'

Selwyn took the packet of letters, and whilst he read Mr. Trosdale busied himself with his models, touching them affectionately, and gazing at them from every side with childlike admiration and pleasure. He was in the act of scrutinizing anxiously a scratch which one model had sustained since he last noticed it, when Selwyn uttered an exclamation of surprise.

'What's the matter?' asked Mr. Trosdale; 'what have you found?'

'Oddly enough, a letter from a man of whom I know something.'

'Who is it?' And Mr. Trosdale came up and peered over his young friend's shoulder. 'Not Anderson? Surely you can't know him?'

'No, Moray. I used to know him very well,' said Selwyn. 'He is the nephew of that Mr. Adams, of Sea Court, of whom you have heard me speak.'

'I remember all about him,' said the older man hastily; 'but why in the name of fortune did you not say you knew this man? Surely you must have been aware that he could be most useful to me!'

'I had quite forgotten for the time that he was in this way of business. And, besides, I didn't feel sure——'

He hesitated slightly, but Mr. Trosdale was too eager to be forbearing.

'Sure of what? Do speak out, and if there's any difficulty in getting at him, let me know it.'

'There is none that I am aware of,' Selwyn answered. 'Mr. Adams was not pleased with something I did a short time ago. But most likely his nephew has not heard of that, and if he has, I don't think it would make much difference. I will go there with you if you like. I see he proposes an appointment.'

'I will write to-night,' said Mr. Trosdale, 'and make an appointment for to-morrow afternoon.'

'Say Monday, for I ought to get leave from Mr. Carthew.'

'Why you will remain where you have to ask for a day out like a servant baffles me. However, let it be Monday. I will go and write the letter now.'

Whilst Mr. Trosdale was thus engaged, Selwyn went down and talked to Madge. He had good news to tell her, for he had heard that morning two Assistant-Surveyors, senior to himself, had received their promotion, thus bringing him perceptibly nearer to his own advancement. Madge received his news with the most sympathetic kindness, and asked so many questions about his prospects, and encouraged him so much, that he longed to ask her whether, when he was promoted and in receipt of an income of £200 a year, she would not let him marry her. He did not venture, however, to put this question when it came to the point; and, after all, the time was only short, for the Surveyor came down at the end of a very few minutes, and under his eyes there was no opportunity for further dallying.

CHAPTER VII.

PARTED.

ON the following morning, when Selwyn came down to breakfast, he found that Mr. Carthew had left a note for him, asking him not to wait, as he had gone out early, and would probably breakfast with a friend in the neighbourhood. Selwyn, therefore, ordered up his eggs and toast, and was leisurely discussing them when Mr. Carthew entered hastily.

'Oh, I'm glad to find you still here,' he said. 'I wanted to see you before we go to the office.'

'What has happened? You seem vexed.'

'Not at all now: rather pleased, in fact, for I have made an arrangement which will satisfy everybody concerned, or I think so. It is about that absurd fellow, Murphy.'

'What about him?' said Selwyn, his curiosity excited to a high pitch. 'I ought to tell you, perhaps, more fully what happened yesterday.'

'Oh, I know! I'm not blind; I saw there was something serious the matter. I did not wish to press my inquiries at the office, since you evidently desired to say nothing more about the quarrel; but I went to Murphy's lodgings last night, and, do you know, he was actually composing a cartel of defiance to be sent to you. A friend of his was helping him, and an extraordinary document it was, I can assure you.'

' Then you saw it ?'

'I did. It was very lengthy, and what with the cramped handwriting, the frequent erasures, and the gutterings from their candle, which more than once obscured a whole line, it was not an easy letter to read. I gathered, however, that Mr. Murphy recommended his friend as one " well versed in the settlement of such disputes, which, having sprung from the interchange of blows, demand the effluence of blood." There was a good deal more which I can't recall. The gist of the matter was that Murphy was thirsting for your gore, and meant to cut "S.S., 1880," beside the initials which his uncle had scrawled on the stock of his pistol.'

'The man must be insane,' said Selwyn contemptuously. 'He was ass enough to strike me, and I naturally knocked him down. There the matter ended, as far as I am concerned.'

'But he took a very different view of it. I sat down and talked to him as reasonably as I could—or rather to his friend, for Murphy declined to discuss the affair with me ; and at last we agreed that the quarrel had originated in a misunderstanding — a decision which Murphy accepted very sullenly. I said I did not think you required any apology, and that the matter might quietly drop.'

'Apology! Good heavens, no !'

'Well, I thought not. But now I've something else to say. Murphy declares he won't return to my office; and his half-witted nephew I don't want. So I've paid them both a week's wages, and they'll not be back any more.'

' I am really vexed,' Selwyn said, ' to have caused you all this annoyance, and the loss of your two clerks.'

' Nonsense! It was not your fault. And I don't honestly think they are much loss. However, we must put our backs into the work, and I shall hand over all the callers to you.'

This threat the Surveyor carefully put into execution, and for some time he remained shut up in his own room the whole day, leaving Selwyn to wrestle with the taxpayers. The experience which he had gained in Liverpool made this comparatively easy to him, and on the whole he enjoyed the work.

On the day appointed with Mr. Trosdale he accompanied him to the offices of Anderson, Moray, and Co. He had received a very friendly note from Mr. Moray, referring to former days in which they had met at Sea Court, and especially to one fine June morning, on which he and Selwyn had gone out whiffing for mackerel together; expressing the greatest interest in any scheme which he had contrived, and concluding with a reproachful hint that Selwyn should not have

been in London for any length of time without looking him up. The note was so friendly,
and the writer’s kind intention so manifest,
that Trosdale, to whom Selwyn showed it,
was greatly exalted, and soared at once into
the most ethereal regions of anticipation. It
was marvellous how great a change was
worked in the ex-Surveyor by an event to
which a sane man would have attached very
small importance. He had been for several
days gradually sinking into the depth of dejection, only roused by Selwyn’s visits, which in
some vague way inspired him with fresh confidence, but quickly relapsing into his former
state when his young coadjutor had gone.
He refused all comfort, he declined to allow
Madge to speak to him on the subject of
what he was beginning to call his ‘ wrongs ;’
he, who was naturally courteous to his
servants, even cursed the poor little lodging-
house drudge in language which, as she said
with flaming cheeks, ‘ no flesh could abear.’
In short, disappointment was having the
worst possible effect on Mr. Trosdale, and
his better nature seemed completely hidden.

It was a little thing, this letter from Mr.

Moray, to work such an improvement in the spirits of a man to whom it was not addressed. The goodwill, such as its practical value might be, was exhibited towards Selwyn, and Selwyn only. But it was characteristic of Mr. Trosdale that the bond which united his interests with those of his former Assistant was in his mind capable of being tightened or relaxed just as circumstances should dictate. It was 'we' or 'I' as might be advisable at the moment; and when the chances of success seemed brightest, 'I' was most frequently in Mr. Trosdale's mouth. It was 'I' who was to grant Selwyn a liberal salary in consideration of his abandoning his official career in order to devote himself solely to his patron's interests; it was 'we' who, as such roseate visions paled and became obscured with clouds, were to go together to Mr. Moray, and by the exercise of every art of seduction persuade him to purchase the furnace.

As soon as this was decided, Mr. Trosdale cast off his anxiety and dejection like a cloak. He became gay and even jocular, rallied Madge on the paleness of her cheeks, and promised to take her to Richmond on the following afternoon. He plied Selwyn hard with questions about Mr. Moray, making him repeat his answers over and over again, and expressing the most unqualified approval of everything he said. Selwyn feared he was building too confidently on success, and told him so.

'I am half afraid you will be disappointed in Mr. Moray,' he said; 'he has always been very kind to me; but then, you see, I have never approached him on his business side.'

'He would not be very ready to talk of business to an inexperienced lad, I can well understand,' rejoined the ex-Surveyor loftily; 'but that does not prove I need anticipate disappointment.'

'No, no,' answered Selwyn, good-temperedly enough; 'but I meant more than that; I have just a doubt in my own mind whether he is quite as pleasant in business as in private life. I fancy he may be harder; he is certainly very prompt in forming a judgment.'

'Promptness is the very quality I love,' Mr. Trosdale answered; 'if he is only prompt we shall get on.'

Selwyn shook his head doubtfully, and the conversation dropped.

Mr. Moray had specially requested that they would bring with them only plans of the furnace; adding that he remembered what skill Selwyn had in drawing mechanical details, and was confident his young friend could represent with his pencil all that it was requisite in this preliminary visit to show. Afterwards they could examine the model, if the first interview should render it advisable to do so. Mr. Trosdale pished a good deal over this; but was consoled when Madge pointed out that the model had already suffered from being carried about from place to place, and that it would be better for Mr. Moray to come and see it in Frith Street.

'It's likely enough he'll want to come at once,' observed the sanguine inventor, as he set out, 'so hold yourself in readiness, child.'

Madge, standing at the window, watched the two figures disappear round the corner into Soho Square with a curious feeling of dread. For a little while she could not define the sensation even to herself: but the idea was constantly recurring to her mind that at some time, some long past time, a girl young as she herself was had stood at the same window watching for calamity. She·threw her whole strength into the effort to shake off this impression: it was too strong for her. She told herself that in the years which had gone by since the house was built, many generations had dwelt in it, and that tidings both good and ill must have been many times borne thither. It was no strange matter, she thought, if some young maiden, whose heart-strings were wrung with anxiety and fear, had watched from the window at which she stood : there was nothing in such a circum-stance to alarm her; it was but that in domestic history events repeated themselves. How many joyful events might have happened in the same spacious room!—the happy meetings of long parted friends ; jovial dinner-parties ; dances ; entertainments of all kinds, from which sadness was banished, and lights and music chased away anxiety. What con-fidences the old walls must have heard ! How many secrets could they not have told ! Even the half-whispered promise which bound two lives together might have been uttered more than once in the old room since the time when the builders left it, and its painted ceiling looked fresh and bright in the sunshine of those days, ere London smoke and fogs had tarnished its colours.

It was useless, however, for Madge to endeavour to distract her thoughts by following out such reflections as these. Her mind was in truth sorely overstrained. Want of proper food and of mental peace were telling on her vigorous constitution; and she could now no more restrain her morbid imaginations than she could procure success for her father's invention. However bravely she strove to turn her thoughts, the idea of the girl so like herself, standing watching at the window, still recurred to her; till at last, feeling something like a nervous terror, she went downstairs, and brought up her landlady's youngest child, a chubby, rosy-faced boy of four, who had struck up a great friendship with her during her stay in Frith Street.

The child demanded a fairy-tale, and Madge told him the story of the girl who lay sick in the winter time, crying for strawberries; and of her kind-hearted playmate who set off alone through the snow in search of them, and of the wonderful adventures by which she found them, and brought them home to her sick friend. After that she told the boy one story after another, till at last he fell asleep with his curly head on her arm.

Madge did not move for fear of waking him; but she noticed that evening was coming on, and that her father and Selwyn must have been away some hours. What could be detaining them? Was it a good sign or a bad one that they were absent so very long?

At last there was a footfall on the stairs, a slow despondent step; but though Madge listened intently, she could not detect the sound of a second person following the first.

Why was one returning without the other? She had barely time to ask herself this question, when the door opened, and the Surveyor entered with the dejected appearance of a man who has encountered absolute and unexpected failure.

He cast his hat, together with the papers which he carried, on the floor, sat down beside the table, and, with a heavy groan, buried his face in his hands.

For an instant Madge looked at him in absolute terror; then she laid down the child on the sofa, and, putting her arms round her father's neck, exclaimed :

'My darling, tell me what has happened ?'

At the same moment the little boy, thoroughly roused from sleep, began to whimper peevishly.

'Take that brat away,' said the Surveyor, in a hoarse voice; 'his whining maddens me !'

Madge took the child down to his mother, and then, returning to her father's side, repeated her question. He answered only by an inarticulate moan and a convulsive movement of the shoulders, while Madge, in an agony of alarm, took his cold hands in hers, and adjured him with every term of endearment to tell her the cause for this abandonment of grief.

At last Mr. Trosdale raised his head, and showed his daughter a face so haggard and worn as to be scarcely recognisable for that of the self-confident man who had parted from her a few hours before with a boasting remark on his lips.

'It is all over, child,' he said. 'I am ruined!'

'Do not be so much cast down, father,' entreated Madge, scarcely knowing what she was saying; 'all will come right after a little. If Mr. Moray does not care to take up the furnace there are plenty of other people in London, possessed, I dare say, of more influence, who will. You must try to have a good night's sleep and forget this vexation, whatever it is, and in a day or two doubtless you will hear of some one else likely to help you. We need not fear the future in any case. We got on very well before, and we shall no doubt do very well again.'

Though the poor girl spoke so hopefully, her heart sank as she did so, and it cost her an enormous effort to prevent her voice breaking. She knew only too well that the future was very dark, and that even if her father's confidence in himself was renewed the day of reckoning would surely come. Sooner or later he must open his eyes to the fact that he had bartered a good, secure position and a certain income for a shadow without substance.   Might he not, now as well as later, unclasp his hand, and taste at once the bitterness of seeing that it held only withered leaves ?

Mr. Trosdale, it seemed, had not heard his daughter's words ; for he sat staring vacantly before him, as if his mind were withdrawn altogether from what was passing around.   Madge was about to speak again, when he brushed his hand across his forehead as if thrusting away some weight which was galling him, and bent down to pick up the plans which he had thrown on the floor.   He glanced at each of them in turn with a grim face, and then, placing the sheets together, he tore them suddenly across and flung them from him.

'Father!' cried Madge in dismay ; 'Selwyn's plans !'

'Yes, Selwyn's plans,' answered her father savagely.   'Curse them every one !'

As he said this he trod them underfoot with a gesture of concentrated passion, and then turned on his daughter :

'Why don't you ask me where Selwyn is?' he said. 'Aren't you anxious about him? Don't you wonder why I have come back alone? Oh, I won't keep you in suspense. I have no doubt he has gone to dine with his dear friend, Mr. Moray. Aren't you glad?'

'If he is likely to enjoy himself, I am glad, of course,' replied Madge, terribly alarmed, and quite unable to follow the drift of her father's mind; 'but I don't understand you.'

'I'll go bail he will enjoy himself,' went on Mr. Trosdale savagely. 'Why should he not? Moray will give him a good dinner, and probably drive him home in the evening. There will be no long dusty walk for him; neither will there be the aching heart, beside which the greatest weariness of body seems ease.'

As the ex-Surveyor uttered the last words his voice sank very low, and there was in his attitude an absolute dejection that cut Madge to the heart.

'Will you not have something to eat, father?' she said, laying her hand again on his shoulder. 'You are fagged to death. Lean back in your easy-chair, and I will make the tea. We will not talk any more till you are rested.'

'No tea,' answered Mr. Trosdale, leaving the other suggestion unnoticed; 'give me a glass of water—I am parched.'

He drank the water when his daughter fetched it, and then allowed her to place him in a great chair beside the window, which was raised sufficiently to admit the cool evening air. The street had become quiet, and the lamps were already lit. The gleam from one of them shone through the panes, and was sufficient to make everything in the room dimly visible. The haggard features of the man sitting by the window with closed eyes and mouth half open seemed in the faint light yet more pinched and wrung than they really were; his hair appeared whiter, and it might really be that in this sleep of excessive weariness some signs of age were revealed which the play of expression in his face usually hid. If this were not so, Madge must have looked on her father that night with sharpened eyes, for a sudden pang seized her as she observed how old he looked—how much older than his years.

It was too dark for any occupation, and Madge could only sit gazing at her father—thinking, thinking, afraid to move, lest she should rouse him. He lay quite still for a long time, perhaps an hour, and then awoke and sat upright, grasping the arms of the chair with his hands.

'Why are you sitting in the dark?' he asked fretfully.

'I thought you were asleep,' answered Madge, and she lighted the gas and drew the blinds down.

Completely roused, Mr. Trosdale rose and began to walk about the room. He paused at last opposite his daughter, and said :

'It is necessary that you should know what has happened to-day.'

'Don't tell me, father, if it pains you. I can guess that Mr. Moray would not help you.'

'If that were all I should thank God with all my heart. What has occurred is worse, far worse, than any mere temporary disappointment. I would spare you if I could, but you must know, for it concerns you as much as it does me. When we got to Moray's office he was out—at lunch, his clerk thought—though we had called by appointment. That was insolent and a bad beginning. However, we waited half an hour as patiently as we could. At last our gentleman came in, looking cool and airy, and apologising in a careless off-hand way for having kept us waiting. That made my blood boil, and I said something which let him know that I resented his impertinence. He scarcely noticed my remark, but began to talk to Selwyn about Somersetshire. After the pair had ignored my very existence for ten minutes or so, I began to feel it was almost time for me to understand in what light I was regarded there, and whether any business was to be done or not. So I suggested, as coolly as I could, that it might be well to come to the point of our visit. When I spoke, Moray turned round, and said: "Yes, to be sure; let me look at those plans, please." I wanted to explain them, but he seemed to think he knew everything, and took them away to a table beside the window, and turned them over for five minutes, when he said, " I am very sorry to tell you, Mr. Trosdale, that this scheme of yours will never work."'

'Oh ! how could he tell ?' ejaculated Madge.

'Of course,' her father answered wrathfully, 'he could not tell. I said, " Let me observe that you have hardly studied my idea sufficiently to make it possible for you to judge of that." To which he had the audacity to reply that no prolonged examination was necessary, for that he was already acquainted not only with my idea, but with the obstacles to its success. " Obstacles !" I cried ; " why, it has succeeded. Come and see my model." "On a small scale," he said, "on a small scale, Mr. Trosdale. You have not tried it on a large one." " I have not built a furnace as large as Snowdon, if that is what you mean," I replied, " but I have satisfied myself that it *will* work ; and you may take my word for it." He shook his head in a superior kind of way, and said, " I am afraid I must believe my own experience, Mr. Trosdale, in preference to your theory." I saw that it was useless to go on in that way, so I changed my tack, and asked him to mention a few of the obstacles that he saw to the success of my plan. At first he hesitated in a way which seemed to me very odd ; and, when I pressed him hard, he said, quite frankly, that he knew how to overcome some of them, and would prefer to say nothing more on the subject. That showed me at once how the land lay: the man had seized my notion, and meant to make use of it in his own way. So I told him I saw through his game, and that it was a dangerous one to play. I warned him that I would leave no stone unturned to protect my rights, and that he should not pirate my invention without being placarded through the City as a dishonourable scoundrel. He made no answer whatever, but sat looking at me very strangely with a half-smile. Then Selwyn must needs interfere, taking his friend's part against me. I could not stand that, and I got up and called to Selwyn to come away. Well, will you believe that he refused to come ? said he would follow me in a little while ; and Moray at once asked him to dine with him. " I fear, after what has passed, it would be an empty compliment to ask you to join us," he said to me. I replied that it certainly would be. I was just leaving when Moray called after me, " I may as well say, Mr. Trosdale, I have already taken out a patent somewhat similar to yours, and that I have been busily engaged for some time in overcoming the difficulties I spoke of just now." I did not answer him—I could not, for I knew my brain-child had been again stolen.'

' My poor father, my dear father !' murmured Madge, her eyes filled with tears.

' Don't, for God's sake, begin pitying me ! The thing is bad enough without that. This is how I stand. My scheme is in the hands of another man, who has capital and connection. How he got it I don't know. If he was not lying when he said he had already taken out a patent, of course some one must have disclosed my plan to him ; and the only person who could have done so is Serle.'

' Father ! You cannot think he would have done such a thing !'

' But I do ; and that's what breaks my heart. I trusted him so.'

'And you may trust him still!' exclaimed Madge.

'How came Moray, then, to know all about *this* affair? Isn't he Serle's friend? Why does Serle separate himself from me, and stay with Moray? Can't you see it is because he thinks the Scotchman can work out the plan better than I, and he is quite indifferent what becomes of me as long as he prospers himself?'

'There's some terrible mistake here,' said Madge, in an agony. 'Selwyn is no more capable of such an act of treachery than I am.'

'You may believe what you like about the matter,' said her father; 'the evidence of my senses is good enough for me. I never expected you to side with me; you have never been able to pretend even that you had any faith in your father. But I have done with Serle.'

The words were hardly out of his mouth when Selwyn entered the room; and on seeing him, Mr. Trosdale repeated:

'I have done with Serle for ever!'

'May I ask what you mean by saying you

have done with me, sir?' asked the young man. 'I have never given you any cause to cast me off.'

'If I had known you were listening, not for the first time, I should have put my meaning into plainer language,' answered Mr. Trosdale, his face growing white with passion.

'I was not listening. I came direct up-stairs; and it was only as I entered the room that I heard your last remark. Do not be unjust to me, Mr. Trosdale. We have been friends too long to quarrel about this deplorable coincidence.'

'There is no coincidence. You betrayed my secret to that false, insolent Scotchman!'

'I did not.'

'You did—I do not believe your word. The man who would betray me would lie in order to conceal his shame. If you did not tell my secret, explain who did. How did Moray come to know it? Was it revealed to him in a dream?'

Selwyn flushed scarlet at this speech; but he bit his lip, and answered quite calmly:

'He tells me that the notion occurred to

him long ago ; and that an almost similar idea has been in the minds of many other people for a considerable time.   He has himself been trying to perfect it for two years past, but has, as yet, only partially succeeded.'

'He lies !' interrupted Mr. Trosdale furiously.

'I am sure he speaks the literal truth,' rejoined Selwyn.

'He lies, I tell you !' shouted the ex-Surveyor.   'He is a false hound ; and you are in league with him.   The plan is mine, and mine only.   Heaven will curse these scoundrels who are trying to rob me of it !'

He stopped suddenly, for he perceived that Madge had seized Selwyn by the arm, and was motioning to him to leave the room.

' Let him stay !' he cried ; ' he shall not go till I have done with him.'

And the infuriated man set his back against the door, and said :

'Come, now, Serle, pluck up courage, and confess the dirty thing you have done.'

'I have nothing to confess,' answered Selwyn.

'Will you dare to deny that Moray kept

you behind in order to talk over my business ?'

' I might evade that question if I chose,'
Selwyn answered ; ' but I admit Mr. Moray
did talk over your affair with me.'

' Hear him! That's frank at last! We
are getting on now. And by what right did
you discuss my business with a stranger, and
a man whom you knew to be my rival ?'

' I had no authority from you to do so ;
but I do not think it was necessary, seeing
that we have been intimate for so long, and
that the discussion was carried on in the
friendliest tone towards you.'

' Heaven grant me patience ! And what
was decided at this precious interview, in
which you did me the honour to represent
me without my leave, and to talk freely about
my private concerns ?'

' I don't admit your right to use that tone
towards me,' said Selwyn, losing temper at
last. ' You should remember, Mr. Trosdale,
that there are limits to patience. I will tell
you, however, what passed. Mr. Moray explained to me at length what the course of his
own investigations had been ; and he pointed

out to me the fault in your plan, and how it
might possibly be overcome.'

' Tell me now.'

' I am not at liberty to do so at present.'

' A precious partner and assistant you are !
Why don't you admit at once that you told
him all my notions, as I confided them to
you ?'

' You misjudge me,' Selwyn answered, with
an obvious effort at self-control.   ' The conclusion of the matter was that he made a
proposal to me, which I think a generous
one.   It was that you should call on him
again at the end of a week, laying aside in
the meantime all idea of any design on his
part to swindle you.   It might then be possible to discuss the matter temperately, and
to see whether you and he could not work
together, with a view to conquer the faults in
both patents, and arrange, if you succeed,
for some share, ultimately, in the profits.'

' Is it possible that you have the insolence
to convey such a proposal to me ?' asked Mr.
Trosdale, with a look of bewilderment.   ' You
must be insane !'

' Do not reject Mr. Moray's offer without

very careful thought,' implored Selwyn.
' Whatever you may think of me, don't throw
away this chance. I give you my word that
he is much nearer success than yourself.'

' Hear how he pleads for his accomplice !'
laughed the Surveyor, pointing his finger at
his young friend. ' Just let this end, Serle.
You may tell Moray, from me, that I saw to-
day he was a liar and a thief. What you tell
me now convinces me that he is a sharp-
witted and plausible one. You have proved
yourself his equal in every way. I will have
no more to do with either of you—and I
hope I may never see you again. It was an
evil day for me when you came to Liverpool.
I gave you all I had to give. I admitted you
to my home. I intrusted you with my plans.
I confided in you in every way—and nobly
you have repaid me. Well, this will be a
lesson to me throughout life. Leave my
house now for ever, and take with you the
consolation of having succeeded in bringing
about the absolute ruin of one who trusted
you. I congratulate you on the skill with
which you have effected your object.'

He opened the door ; then, seeing that

Madge was stretching out her hands, with an imploring gesture, towards Selwyn, he said, not without a touch of feeling :

'I am going upstairs for ten minutes. Do not give me the pain of finding you here when I return.'

Before the ten minutes expired Selwyn had left the house in Frith Street, and Madge was kneeling beside the bed in her own room, sobbing as if her heart would break.

CHAPTER VIII.

'OH ! MY LOST LOVE.'

THERE are times in the lives of all of us on which we never care to look back—times of agonized sorrow, of deep humiliation, of horrible disappointment, of loss, of temptation, of loneliness, of struggle, of sin, of unavailing repentance, of anguish too full of remorse for tears. There is scarce a single person that has arrived at middle manhood who can truthfully say there is not one leaf, at all events, in the book of his existence he would fain forget.

To Selwyn Serle the months which followed after his parting interview with Mr. Trosdale will always seem like a bad nightmare. Till the end of his life he will never be able to recall the sequence of hopeless days and weary nights he then spent without a shudder—never, so long as for him grass grows and water flows will he be able to speak, even to his nearest and dearest, of what he went through while his torn heart was recovering from wounds such only as can be inflicted by those we have loved and trusted.

He had loved and trusted Mr. Trosdale. His own dimly-remembered father could have occupied no higher place in his esteem and affection. Of the best he had in him he had given to his friend. What, indeed, had he not given cheerfully, thankfully, joyfully!

The spring-time of youth, which to a man comes not twice—the hope, the energy, the faith, the help unselfishly offered and gladly received—all these things he laid before Mr. Trosdale as things of naught, asking for nothing in exchange.

As for the money lost so utterly, Selwyn took no account of it consciously. Had it been double, treble the amount he never would have grudged parting with it; but still, insensibly even to himself, his poor hundreds went to swell the sum-total of an account in which to him there had been no profit.

For the one possession he might have saved from the wreck was relentlessly swept from him. Even Madge had passed out of his life, and the sweetness of the days of poverty and trial they faced so happily together was turned into bitterness.

Death, poor lad, he thought he could have borne better. Around the memory of his dead there hung no chaplet of rue. All connected with them was calm as their quiet resting-place, but he could associate nothing calm or restful with his parting from Madge.

He knew her well. She had said she believed in him utterly—God bless her for that belief!—nevertheless——

'We will say good-bye now, my darling, for ever;' and she kissed him, weeping sore, but still had strength to make him go.

She did not believe—had never believed—in her father. 'But he is my father, Selwyn, so my first duty is to him; for whom has he in all the wide world beside me?'

He had no one. He never could have anyone so near, so faithful, who would bear with him, be true to him, patient, helpful, long-suffering, kind.

'Should the day ever come that he finds out how cruelly he has wronged me, you will send for me at once, will you not?'

'Yes—should the day ever come; but that day will never come. Put us out of your life; and try to make the good thing of it you might, if we had never met.'

If they had never met! There were times when, in his deep despondency, Selwyn wished they never had. Spite of crosses and losses, he was happy in the old days that seemed so far away; happy before Mr. Trosdale 'took to him,' and hopeful too. But, oh! he had been happier since. And, as he recalled his walks with Madge to Cleveland Square; the evenings they loitered under the windows of St. George's Hall; the services they both attended in St. Paul's Church—ah, there was one service he once thought would be held in that church for them alone!—the never-to-be-forgotten little excursions down the river; the funny parties they had made so merry over—he felt as if his heart must break to think everything that once seemed fresh, and fair, and beautiful was dead as last year's flowers, and had left no fruit except what was sour as wild grapes, and bitter as aloes.

'Oh, my love—my own lost love!' that was the refrain his weary soul kept for ever chanting.

Not even when his spirit waxed hottest within him had he a hard thought towards her.

He never believed she would cease to care for him, and learn to care for anyone else. The idea that another might win and wear her did not enter his mind. He pictured her through the years still ministering to and bearing with her father, who, wrapped up in himself and his own foolish, selfish concerns, would not even understand, much less be grateful, for the sacrifice she made.

When his reflections reached this point Selwyn felt possessed with a sort of fury. These moods generally came upon him after office hours, and he would seize his hat and rush out and walk for miles, in a vain striving to lay the devil which mastered him.

That such a life as Madge's should be

utterly wasted, as he considered the matter, drove him almost frantic.

'Anybody,' he said in his wrath, 'who saw his meals were well cooked and his clothes mended, would serve her father's turn as well as Madge—why should she be sacrificed? It does not signify about me; if I knew she was happy I should not mind being miserable myself.' And yet all the time, poor lad, he was minding being miserable, very much indeed—mentally asking why such a burden had been put upon him—why, out of the whole world, he had been the person selected as a scape-goat to bear the whole weight of Mr. Trosdale's follies and crimes.

'For a man who does everything he ought not, and nothing that he ought, is as much a criminal as any felon living in Newgate;' which was putting the case strongly, yet perhaps not too strongly.

When Selwyn went to London, which was often, he always managed—no matter in which direction his business lay—to pass through Frith Street, not once, but many times; but never did a sight of his lady-love gladden his eyes. There was the house, but

her face never appeared at the window.
Going, or coming, or sauntering up and
down, he never met her, never caught even a
glimpse of her in the distance.

Fate evidently had a spite against him.
Other people quite by accident ran up
against those they desired to see; but he,
though he sought her sedulously, was never
so happy as in the morning, or at noon, or
evening, to meet her even for a moment.

How was it that no chance threw him
across her path, that he always failed to time
his quick or loitering footsteps to the happy
minute when they might keep glad tune with
hers?

She had not used to be such a stay-at-
home. In St. Paul's Square any beggar
might have seen her a dozen times a day;
and now he who only craved for a smile, a
look, for even a sight of her shadow as she
passed, had always to return to his desolate
lodgings empty and faint, sick at heart, and
lonely beyond description.

One day, nine months after their bitter
parting, when, after fruitlessly pacing up and
down the street, he was about to turn away

in despair, he saw a servant going on some
errand.   It was not the same servant he had
known, but in a lodging-house there is not
much use in taking account of changes in
servants.   She came out of the door he had
so often entered ; that was enough for him,
and he followed and came up with her before
she reached Soho Square.

'How is Miss Trosdale?' he asked.

The girl looked at him sharply.   She
was but a poor little drab-of-all-work,
wearing a new hat much too small for her,
old boots—which originally belonged to some
far bigger person—as much too large, and
an amazing Piccadilly fringe ; but she was a
past-mistress in that style of brilliant repartee
which shines in such sentences as :

'It's manners not to speak till you're asked,
ain't it ?   Perhaps you're not aware who you
are addressing of.'

'Keep your distance, please.   Nobody
wants you to lessen it.'

'Perhaps you mistake me for your Sal ; but
she never gets out, except on Sunday evenings, after all the family is gone to bed.'

One of twenty such phrases trembled on

the poor little hussy's lips (we must all have our own consolations, and there must be a consolation in dialogue of this description, or else it would not obtain to the extent it does), but as she looked at Selwyn they all died away.

Here was no toff, no lardy-dardy swell, no blackguard in her own class of life, no scoundrel such as infests even at high noon—at high noon, indeed, more than at high night—our London streets ; nobody in answer to whose signal it was necessary to run up the flaunting flag of female virtue, which frequently serves its owner the scurvy trick of hauling itself down at the first suggestion of siege.   Only an ' ordinary ' young man who meant no harm, and who thought she was somebody else, instead of Catherine Jane Herser, who combined in her own bewitching person the various characters of cook, housemaid, chambermaid, parlourmaid, shoeblack and drudge to Mrs. Lovell.

' I knows no Miss Trosdale,' she answered, with more urbanity of manner than her words might suggest.

' But you came out of Mrs. Lovell's, surely——'

' Mrs. Lovell ain't Miss Trosdale, is she ?'

' No ; I mean the young lady who lodges with her.'

' There ain't no young lady lodging along of her—neither has there been in my time.'

' And how long has your time been ?'

' Going on for three months. See here— do you want to know very much about the young lady ?'

' Certainly. Why do you ask ?'

' Because I shan't be more nor five minutes away ; and if you'd wait till I come back, I could ask where is she gone.'

' Thank you greatly ; but I can ask my-self.'

' Oh ! I have no wish to put myself for-ward. Sorry I spoke ; but my intention was good.'

' I am sure it was,' said Selwyn ; ' but I have spoken to Mrs. Lovell often. She knows who I am, and will tell me where Miss Trosdale is to be found. I feel obliged to you all the same, however.' And he slid half-a-crown into the girl's hand, which did not close on it.

On the contrary, she held it out on her

palm, and Selwyn could not help noticing how black and grimed that palm was. Her dirt struck him with a sense of pity. It was, indeed, almost pathetic.

'What's this for?' she asked.

'To buy whatever you like with,' explained Selwyn. 'I have given you some trouble.'

'I wouldn't mind taking a good deal more at the same price,' returned the girl, in a spirit of light and playful satire. 'Well, if you are sure you won't let me ask for you——'

'Quite sure,' put in Selwyn.

'I had best be going on my errand,' which she immediately did, while Selwyn retraced his steps to the well-remembered house.

'Yes, it was true,' Mrs. Lovell told him; 'Mr. and Miss Trosdale had left more than six months; and sorry enough she was to lose such good lodgers.'

Did she know where they had gone? Well, Miss Trosdale did say—yes, and wrote it down, too; because she showed the address to that stout gentleman, who copied it into his pocket-book. Had she the direction still? She thought so; but there's so many things to attend to. However, if Mr. Serle would step inside, she would look. He had been away, she supposed. Perhaps he would like to wait in the rooms while she made search for the piece of paper—she knew what it was like—she could remember it the minute her eyes lit on it—and, dear—dear! had he been for all this weary time where he could neither see nor hear from that dear young lady? It must have seemed a terrible while to him! And if he knew of any friends who wanted comfortable apartments, she hoped he would bear hers in mind. She would not mind making a reduction to parties recommended by him. It did seem home-like and natural to see him standing just where he had stood so often. He would excuse her leaving him while she found the address? And so she went away at last, and left Selwyn free to look round the dingy room where he had known such happiness, out of which he had gone feeling more utterly wretched than at any time during the whole of his life.

It all returned to him with a rush, as a great wave of memory came sweeping over his soul, and when the waters ebbed he saw stranded all he had hoped—all he had lost.

It was but a year and nine months since that wet day in August when he strode, strong of heart and high of courage, under his dripping umbrella, sad and sorrowful when he thought of the good, peaceful, happy past, but confident that the future held for him much he should still prize and enjoy.

As in a dream, he saw that young fellow plodding cheerily along through the rain, and felt a pang of regret to think he could never so plod cheerily again. Not two years ago he had first seen Mr. Dandison, and obtained his credentials in the form of that letter to Mr. Trosdale!

It was a short time in which to have made such a shipwreck of his life. He had gone to Liverpool determined to do his duty ; determined to be brave, honest, proud of a name which had never yet been linked with disgrace, careful as to his associates, mindful of all the tender home lessons, the kindness of old friends, the wisdom of his elders—and he had kept his good resolution to the best of his ability. Nevertheless, reviewing the past in Mrs. Lovell's front parlour, he despairingly considered the result could scarcely have proved worse had he spent the time since that inclement Monday in folly and riot.

When the columns of his experience came to be added up, what was the sum-total? Loss! He had loved and lost, been faithful and deemed false, been the truest of friends and considered the worst of traitors.

And, on the other side, what advantage had he gained? The memory of a girl which would sadden his life. Ah! that was not all sadness. To think of Madge was to think of some one far beyond personal selfishness as the heaven is high above the earth. If they never met again—if never for ever he heard her voice nor touched her hand, nor looked in those eyes which had once so perplexed him, he knew he ought, after having known her, to walk through the world nobler, stronger, because of the nobility and the strength in her.

What if there had come a coldness betwixt himself and the kind friends at Sea Court; what if all old things had passed away, and no new experiences which were pleasant seemed ever likely to arise; what if he had grown less hopeful, less cheerful, more lonely, more heart-weary ?—still—still he had known Madge. In that very room had he not constantly seen some evidence of her courage and devotion. Ah, yes! he was wrong to complain. There is a goal even here below more to be desired than ease and pleasure, and she had shown him the straight path to it.

He thought of her as she knelt that evening all alone in St. Paul's Church, to outward seeming a quiet, prayerful figure ; now, as he understood, a girl solitary beyond expression, wrestling with her sorrow, seeking for strength, striving through darkness to see light.

'My love! shall I be weaker than you were then ?' And the poor fellow's eyes were dim, as the past, with its glamour of beauty, displaced for a moment the hard reality of his bitter present. He was pacing the Liverpool streets again by her side—walking in the moonlight back from Mrs. Gibbs' wonderful party—standing in St. Paul's Square, feeling his first pang of jealousy, when Mrs. Lovell's voice recalled him to London and Soho.

'I have kept you a long while, Mr. Serle,

but — better late than never.   Here it is : Doughty Street, Mecklenburgh Square, near the Foundling.   You'll give my duty to Miss Trosdale, won't you, sir ? and say, whenever she is passing, I should be proud to see her. She was looking a bit peaky before they left me.   The old gentleman was often peevish, and she did not go out enough.   Young people are best in homes of their own—leastways that is my opinion.   But, law ! where is the lot or station without a cross in it somewhere ? I am sure I have had mine.   And if ever you should hear of any newly-married couple wanting apartments, I would do my best to make them comfortable ; and as to terms, we shouldn't quarrel over a shilling or two——'

The contrast between the home he had pictured and Mrs. Lovell's rooms was absurd enough, yet Selwyn could not smile as it occurred to him.   His heart felt full as it could hold, and he stretched out his hand to the landlady without a word.

'I wouldn't let my spirits down, sir, if you can help it, Mr. Serle,' she said.   'You'll excuse me, sir, but I always suspected something had come between you.   Love wouldn't be love, though, if its course ran quite smooth ; and it won't be long, I hope, before I see you and Miss Trosdale walking in here husband and wife, and happy as the day is long.'

'I am glad she said that,' Selwyn muttered to himself, as he sped away straight to Doughty Street; 'though she ought not to have said it, I am glad she did.' And then his pace slackened. After all, why was he rushing off in such hot haste to the north-east— what did he mean to do when he reached Mr. Trosdale's lodgings ? He could not call— he could not ask to see Madge in defiance of her father's prohibition. Why was his soul rejoicing within him—what piece of good fortune had come since he sauntered up and down before a house where his dearest one was not ? He did not know. Something in his life had changed within the last hour ; the weary, stupid calm of despair had lasted long enough. A quickening of his pulse, a more rapid throbbing of his heart, told him some change was imminent.

When would it come, and how ? what form would it assume ? He might not hasten its advent, but he could at least take one step to meet it by asking at the door in Doughty Street, to which he had been directed, how Mr. and Miss Trosdale were.

CHAPTER IX.

'MR. TROSDALE, sir? no, he is not here now. He went, I suppose, ten weeks ago. No, sir, I don't know where he is gone; but I will ask Miss Lewis.'

As it turned out, Miss Lewis did not know either. Mr. Trosdale had been ailing somewhat, and she rather thought he and his daughter had gone to the seaside. She never heard Miss Trosdale say where they were going; they had left no address to which any letters could be forwarded—in fact, only one letter for them had come to Doughty Street since the morning they left. Miss Lewis said she was very sorry she could give so little information. Mr. Trosdale was not in bad health when he left; he only seemed a little out of sorts. The east winds had tried him very much, as, indeed, they had Miss Lewis herself, who wished very much she could get away for a change. Miss Trosdale was quite well, only anxious about her papa, as was natural; not that there was anything to be anxious about, but when daughters were attached to their parents, of course they always thought that if but a finger ached the doctor ought to be sent for. Yes, a doctor had been sent for. Dr. Higgins in Brunswick Square, a very nice gentleman, who had attended many of Miss Lewis' lodgers—in fact, had attended Miss Lewis' aunt in her last illness. She did not think it likely, however, that Dr. Higgins would know where Mr. Trosdale had gone, but it could do no harm to ask him. There was no need to thank her, Miss Lewis declared. She always felt glad to oblige; all she wished was she had been able to tell more.

If that change Selwyn had been certain was impending were approaching, it seemed vain to speculate on its course. What could be the reason, he marvelled, for so many removals? Did Mr. Trosdale desire to take his daughter utterly beyond his (Selwyn's) reach? It might be so, but, on the other hand, why did he pursue such a line of conduct till his commands were infringed? The lovers had not transgressed by word or sign. Why then should Mr. Trosdale choose to vanish so utterly that not even a footprint remained by which to trace him?

Pshaw! the doctor would know all about it. He had ordered his patient most probably to some seaside resort.

'No,' said that gentleman when the question was put to him, 'I have not an idea where Mr. Trosdale is gone, or why he left Doughty Street. I attended him, yes. He was a little low and nervous, but in such cases beef-tea and tonics work wonders. He soon got well; wonderfully soon, for he is not a young man, you must remember. If he has really gone to the seaside I should say it is not for his health, more likely for amusement; time seemed to hang very heavily on his hands. He had no interests, so far as I could judge. He seemed lost in London, quite out of his element; and speaking of that reminds me. Do you not think it is probable they have returned to Liverpool? Miss Trosdale said to me more than once she was heartily sorry they had ever left it.'

'To Liverpool!' repeated Selwyn, amazed. 'I hardly imagine Mr. Trosdale would like to go back to Liverpool. It is a place he always declared he hated.'

'Nevertheless, you may depend it is there you will find him. He was very tired of London.'

Selwyn pondered over this statement till he grew half inclined to believe the doctor right. It was not impossible that, after his disappointment, Mr. Trosdale might have become disgusted with London, and desirous of leaving it. Madge had never taken kindly to the move. She was lonely in London; she disliked lodgings; she could not have matters so comfortable for her father as she wished. Yes, though the idea seemed preposterous at the first blush, the more Selwyn thought over the matter, the more convinced he became that the Surveyor, having failed

to find a fortune in London, had returned to
Liverpool to live on his pension.

He would write to Liverpool and inquire.
No; on second thoughts, he would not write
to anyone—he would go ; and the following
Saturday afternoon, therefore, found him *en
route* for Lancashire.

It was with a strange and miserable sensation he paced the familiar streets next day.
After we have been separated for some time
from even the dearest friend, we find, on
meeting once again, that he is a little strange
to us. A change has passed over him as well
as over us ; but of the one we are conscious.
of the other unconscious. He is not exactly
the friend we remember. The tone of his
voice, the look in his eyes, the smile flitting
around his mouth, his manner, mien, carriage,
are not quite what we imagined ; and in precise proportion generally to the desire with
which we desired to see him, is the vague
disappointment that he is not exactly the
man from whom we parted.

It is much the same with a town which we
have learned to like ; we revisit and grow
gradually to hate it. Not even had his first

sight of Liverpool, in a pouring, pelting rain, exercised so depressing an influence upon Selwyn as its aspect on a bright Sunday morning in May, with the sun flaring down on the pavement, dust blowing round every corner in a playful and childlike manner, the bells clanging out their imperative summons to obedient worshippers streaming along, each bound to the conventicle he specially favoured.

Selwyn went to St. Paul's. If he had any hope that he might there catch a glimpse of Madge, it was disappointed. A man sat at the organ, and among the sparse congregation there was no one who in the least resembled her. After service, the sextoness, who had greeted him on his entrance with a surprised and carefully modulated smile, slid round to the door by which he was leaving, and ventured humbly to hope that Miss Trosdale was well and enjoying her health in London.

In London! So the sextoness evidently had not seen her in Liverpool; but perhaps Mr. Trosdale had taken a house in the suburbs, at too great a distance for his daughter to attend the dreary stranded church situate in a drearier and more stranded square.

'Thank you,' said Selwyn, as one in a dream; 'she was quite well when I saw her last;' and he glanced back at the Communion rails, before which, in fancy, he had so often stood with Madge, hearing the words spoken that meant they should never separate again till death parted them. And now they were parted, and not by death.

'You are not looking quite yourself, sir,' said the woman, a little curious. 'London does not suit you so well as Liverpool.'

'I am not in London, but four miles from it,' he answered.

'Ah! it's all the same,' rejoined the woman. 'None of that south part is healthy—breeds fevers and agues and such like.'

Selwyn shivered as he turned away. He knew the woman's talk was all nonsense about fevers and agues, but he could not tell where his darling might be, or whether she was suffering physically. While he was foolishly taking it for granted she still remained in Soho, what might not have been happening elsewhere? Why had he allowed himself to be parted from her ? Why did he not insist, at least, on an occasional letter ? The midday sun was streaming straight down on the graveyard as he left St. Paul's, touching the old tombstones with shafts of brightness, and even rendering some of the inscriptions legible to the passer-by ; but the sunshine could not warm Selwyn's chilled heart. He felt as if an icy hand were clutching it. He could know no rest or happiness till he found Madge and satisfied himself she was well.

When he came to the old house where he had known such fulness of happiness he paused for a moment—it was tenanted. A residence of that description in the heart of the town, and close to the river, was not likely to remain vacant for long, and Selwyn knew this ; nevertheless, it was with an unreasonable pang of regret he saw short blinds at the windows, the outer door set wide, and inner swing-doors for the convenience of people who were constantly entering and leaving.

It did not need a mingled odour of cabbage-water, roast-beef, boiled dumplings, onions, and a broad brass plate bearing the one word

'Radford,' to assure him it was a boarding-house. He could have better borne to see it empty, falling to decay; the fresh paint, the spruce white curtains, the hearth-stoned steps, the flower-pots red-ochred till they made the eye ache, poured the last drop in his cup. An old age of poverty and neglect would have seemed trying enough, but the rakish assumption of youth, the smug look of those red pots filled with musk and creeping jenny, the whited-sepulchre appearance given by those short blinds ornamented with brass rods, made him heart-sick. A little girl in a wonderful pink frock and a little boy dressed in a sailor's suit were running in and out of the hall and pursuing each other along the pavement.

Selwyn would have liked to knock their heads together and change their yells of delight into howls of pain; though he had but just come out of church, he was in a very unchristian humour.

No child likes to see another child in possession of its toys; and, after all, what are houses and land but toys to children of a larger growth?

'I hope I shall never enter this place again,' thought Selwyn ungratefully; and so he left St. Paul's Square, and figuratively shook its dust off his shoes.

He meant to call during the course of that afternoon on everyone with whom Madge had been intimate; no great round of visits, but still sufficient to make him decide on not wasting time in partaking of afternoon or high tea anywhere.

It was still too early by a couple of hours for him to start on his quest. Hungry as people, for some inscrutable reason, always are on Sunday, they would one and all at that precise time be ravenously devouring dinner.

He must possess his soul in patience a little longer still; and as he felt he could not touch food if he ordered it, he decided to take a stroll through all the old haunts he had traversed so often with Madge.

Where was now the glamour that had hung over them?—garish and pretentious, or else mean and sordid, they all appeared to his travelled eyes.

He could see nothing imposing about St. George's Hall, quaint in Cleveland

Square, old-fashioned in Duke Street, and stately in that then queer corner of Liverpool —now being utterly modernized and ruined by nineteenth-century warehouses—Wolstenholm Square. The eye makes its own beauty, the heart its own happiness. Selwyn's eye on that Sunday was not open to the influence of beauty, or his heart to any thrill of happiness.

'It is exactly what I first thought it—a hateful place,' he considered; but if Madge had only come in sight, Liverpool would have been the most charming place in all the world.

Instead of Madge, he saw walking along Bold Street the man he would at any other time have gone a mile out of his way to avoid meeting.

As matters were, he went straight on, and so came face to face with Mr. Ashford.

'What—really you!' exclaimed that gentleman, as he shook hands. 'I thought to myself when I first caught sight of you, "That's very like Serle—I wonder where he is;" but I never imagined it was you. I did not expect you would be coming to Liverpool.'

'I did not expect to be coming myself a few days ago,' answered Serle.   'My journey is quite an unexpected one.'

'Well, expected or the reverse, I am very glad to see you.   How did you leave the gay Metropolis ?'

'The gay Metropolis seemed much as usual when I last was there,' said Selwyn.

'Why don't you say, "in its usual,"' asked Mr. Ashford with forced playfulness ; 'that is a good Scotch expression.'

'As I am not Scotch, English has to be good enough for me,' retorted Selwyn somewhat snappishly.

'English has to be good enough for a great many people,' returned Mr. Ashford. 'And how are your friends the Trosdales, Mr. Serle ?'

'They were in "their usual,"' with a bitter smile, 'when I saw them last ; but that is nine months since—nearly ten, indeed.   You can give me much later news, no doubt ?'

'What, have you never seen them since you and the old man had that row ?'

'Never.'

'Where are you stopping ? The Compton !

Then we are nearer my diggings—come in and have a glass of wine.'

Mentally reserving to himself the right to refuse that glass of wine, Selwyn assented to the suggestion. He thought he was now in the straight way to hear news, and he knew at last from whom Mr. Trosdale had learned to talk about 'diggings.' Very strange, indeed, that such a man as Mr. Ashford should have acquired so great an influence over one who certainly had come of decent people, and was once accustomed to the manners and usages of good society.

In the friendly shelter of a room Selwyn had often puzzled himself over this problem ; but now in the full light of a summer's day, in a wide street filled with well-dressed people, who wore their best manners as well as their best clothes, the problem became distracting.

'How long do you stop here ?' asked Mr. Ashford, as they mounted the stairs to his rooms.

'Quite uncertain,' answered Selwyn, who did not mean to tell Mr. Ashford everything.

'Ah, I understand ; you are down on official business !'

Selwyn said neither yea nor nay. Mr. Ashford could think what he pleased. He was not bound to enlighten him.

By this time they were in a cheerful drawing-room, forming one of a suite of four apartments — bathroom, bedroom, dining-room, and the room in which Selwyn found himself.

'You are pleasantly lodged,' he remarked, by way of saying something.

'Yes—the worst of it is, I am not often here to be pleasantly lodged.'

'I suppose you like travelling about, however ; there must be a good deal of variety in such a life.'

'Well, no, there is not. I know the look of every hedge and ditch, every ploughed field and meadow, every river and canal, every town and village my business takes me through, better than I know the Commandments. I am sick of it all. Sick of the firms I travel for—more sick of the firms I travel to. I am sick also of these lodgings you called pleasant just now, though

the rooms are not bad, and the people who
own them are far above the usual lodging-
house set. Fact is, when a man comes to
my time of life he wants a home, not apartments; a place where he can take root—plant
a rose-tree and gather its roses, sow cucum-
ber-seed and eat cucumbers of his own
growing.'

'I should have thought anyone could do
that,' said Selwyn diffidently. His old
country experiences impelled him to answer,
'Any man can do that;' but recent associa-
tions induced him to modify the sentence.

'No, sir, you are wrong,' replied Mr.
Ashford. 'I could not do it alone. Men
can do nothing of that sort by themselves.
We are helpless without *the* woman. As
you are doubtless aware, I am sceptical concerning the Bible; but if anything could
induce me to go in hot and strong for that
publication, it would be the absolute truth,
confirmed by my own experience, which I
find on every page about women. By ourselves we men are able to do nothing worth
anything. Let the better sex (so-called) make
what they can out of that confession.'

And Mr. Ashford took the cigar from between his lips, stretched out his legs, and filled himself another glass of wine.

Selwyn looked across the table, opened his mouth to ask a question; then, thinking better of the matter, closed it.

Mr. Ashford finished his wine at one gulp.

'I know what you were going to say,' he remarked—'"Then why don't you marry?" Those are the words which trembled on your lips this instant, now ain't they?'

'Something very like them,' argued Selwyn, not in the least abashed.

'Now I feel pleased with that,' said Mr. Ashford oratorically, as if addressing a large and sympathetic audience. 'When you know me better—as you will one day, I hope,' he added, descending from his platform and speaking to Selwyn as a single human being, and not as one in the crowd—'you will find nothing succeed with me like frankness.'

'Then, if you do not mind telling me, *why* do you not marry?' asked Selwyn, with a frankness which seemed to indicate that he desired to succeed very well indeed with Mr. Ashford.

'I do not mind telling you in the least, because just now we are in the same predicament. The lady would not have *me*—the father would not have *you*. Make what you will out of that.'

' Do you mean——' began Selwyn.

Although he had known from the beginning whither Mr. Ashford's talk was tending, the fact that he had indicated Madge fairly staggered him.

'Yes, I do. I mean your old flame, Miss Trosdale. Nicely we have both been humbugged—both, I say—though it is harder on me than on you.'

Selwyn did not answer. It seemed to him answer was impossible as comparison.

'Of course you don't agree with me, but, whatever you may think, it is harder,' went on Mr. Ashford argumentatively. 'At your age it is "lightly come, lightly go." To five-and-twenty everything seems possible ; to forty nothing seems possible, save certainty. Now I felt certain—nay, humanly speaking, as you in your cant would phrase it, I was certain of Miss Trosdale, and yet you see where I am.'

'She refused you?'

Selwyn's throat was parched, and his lips were dry, as he spoke; yet he managed to get out the three words of assertion and inquiry.

'She refused me just as her father did you. If she had not, the father would. If the father had not shown you the door, she would——'

'Sir!'

'Oh! sit down again. Heroics and indignation are worse than out of place between men who have been so badly treated. We are, for the nonce, in the same boat, and we may as well row together for a little while, though, as Douglas Jerrold said, not with the same sculls.'

'If you intend an impertinence, Mr. Ashford, I am absolutely indifferent—you cannot touch me.'

'No—since *she* rejected *me*. If she had not——'

'She *must* have refused you!' retorted Selwyn, stung to the quick. 'There is no "if" in the matter. It is an absolute impossibility Miss Trosdale could ever have accepted you!'

'Ah! you are alluding to the difference in age; but you have no experience. If you knew more of the world you would pooh-pooh that as a mere nothing. I am nineteen years older than Madge Trosdale.' Selwyn clenched his hand. 'When a girl is fifteen and a man thirty-four, of course such a disparity seems enormous; but each year after that things get more equal.'

'Perhaps so,' scoffed Selwyn.

'Of course so,' answered Mr. Ashford. 'At eighteen a woman is in her prime. Each day she lives single after that she deteriorates. You smile incredulously, Mr. Serle; but you are so very young—even for your age you are so very young.'

'Young or not,' retorted Mr. Serle, 'I am glad to remember it is not nineteen years that place a barrier between Miss Trosdale and myself.'

'Is there so much to be thankful for?' retorted Mr. Ashford. 'Remember I am not asserting anything. I am merely asking a question. Except theoretically, is it very charming to be young, to have always to be taking back-seats in the world's synagogues, to have no influence, no position, no money ? In the case of a young duke or a young millionnaire, I can understand the advantage of being one-and-twenty ; but in our rank, where is the benefit ?'

'You must have forgotten your own feelings at one-and-twenty, or you would scarcely ask such a question,' replied Selwyn.

'Pardon me, it is precisely because I do remember what my life then was, that I put the inquiry.   Up in the morning by five ; out to work at six, cold and tired ; often wet, and always hungry ; too weary when the day's labour ended to enjoy the hour's leisure which came in the evening ; poor as a church mouse. No, thank you !   Let those praise youth who have money and leisure to enjoy it.   To the most of people, what is early life but a constant desire for something you can never get ? Take your own case.   Like all Government clerks, you are under-worked and over-paid, yet you don't know what it is to call your soul your own.   You dare not say it is your own for fear of offending a self-sufficient old fool like Trosdale, or an overbearing brute like Cramsey.   And Trosdale and Cramsey are in exactly the same boiling :

‘ “ For great fleas have little fleas
  Upon their backs to bite ’em ;
And little fleas have lesser fleas,
  And so *ad infinitum.*”

The sense of which is, throughout the service, whether you are high or low, there is somebody to take a nip out of you.’

‘ I am very well content with the service.’

‘ I don’t doubt you in the least,’ said Mr. Ashford, with a sneer. ‘ “ Your mind to you a kingdom is.” ’

‘ I could scarcely go so far as that,’ answered Selwyn, who had discovered the way to vex Mr. Ashford was to keep his own temper, ‘ By-the-bye, where is Mr. Trosdale living now ?’ he added, taking a sudden resolution to put this question.

‘ I cannot tell you.’

‘ Does “ cannot ” stand for “ will not ”? ’

‘ No. My severance from your old chief, though more recent than your own, is quite as complete.’

‘ Yet I thought you and he were great friends ?’

‘ Well—yes—once. When I could be of use to that clever individual, there was no one so dear a friend to Mr. Trosdale as your humble servant. The moment. however, he found no more money was to be got out of me, he showed himself in his true colours. Fact is, he would ruin his father and dishonour his mother, if those excellent people were still alive, for the sake of that misshapen offspring of his brain, the furnace.'

'But you always were urging him to proceed with it.'

'So I was, till I found he knew no more of science, or smelting, or furnace, or any other useful thing, than the babe unborn. His invention is all rot! It is the old business—what is new about it is not true, and what is true isn't new ; in other words, anything in the whole matter which has any merit is not his own, and what is his own might as well be the plan of anyone else, because it is useless. Do you see ?'

'Not exactly ; but I suppose you mean the furnace is doomed to failure.'

'It was doomed to failure from the first ; but I, of course, could not tell that. How was I to know the man, who professed to be able to box the whole compass of science, was really a silly pretender, duped by his own inordinate vanity, and willing to beggar friend and foe able to advance money to prolong the life of his accursed abortion even for a week ?'

' You speak very strongly——'

' Not half so strongly as I feel. It is no fault of his that I am not a ruined man. Old idiot ! He would sit for hours—for weeks—purring, while anybody stroked his vanity ; but the moment a friend tried to tell him some plain truths he would show his claws, and fly at the venturesome individual tooth and nail. Once upon a time he desired nothing better than that I should marry Missie. When he knew I did not intend to marry his patent too, he joined with her and against me. I see the whole matter now — father and daughter were always in league ; there is no truth in either of them.'

' I cannot listen to such a remark.'

' I beg your pardon. I forgot you are not yet disillusioned. It seems strange, too ; for Miss Trosdale told me she was thankful you had cut yourself adrift from them.'

' You must have misunderstood her,' said

Selwyn. ' It was not I who cut myself adrift, but Mr. Trosdale who sent me adrift.'

' Yes—over that Moray affair ? If it had not been that, it would soon have been something else. He had long been getting tired of you. Bless you, I wasn't in the least surprised when I heard the crash had come ! I was only astonished to find you took his dismissal so quietly.'

' How was it possible for me to take it otherwise ?'

' Well—unless you really did blab his secrets—perhaps you did, though ; it seems you attempted no explanation.'

' It is not easy to explain when one's letters are returned unopened.'

' Why did you not insist on seeing him ?'

' I could not force myself into a man's house against his will.'

' There is something in that. Couldn't Moray have cleared you ?'

' If Mr. Trosdale wouldn't believe me, he would not believe Mr. Moray.'

' So long as the fit is on him he would not believe anybody. But I don't know that it much signifies. It is a good thing for you to have done with him. He is not a man to advance your interests in the service. He has done you a lot of harm as it is.'

' I do not think that at all, Mr. Ashford.'

' But I know it,' was the uncompromising reply. ' Look here, you haven't been frank with me, still I'll be frank with you. Business never brought you to Liverpool. You came to find out Trosdale's address, which I can't tell you, for I have had no communication with him since I got my dismissal. But there is a man out at East Greenwich who has had a great deal to do with your friend lately. Together they have been trying to discover why the deuce the furnace won't work. Very likely he can tell you where Trosdale is living. Matheson, Engineer, East Greenwich. Now, don't thank me. I am doing you anything but a kindness ; only, a " wilful man must have his way "—and a foolish one too, for that matter. Moray has abandoned his scheme as impracticable. If you can induce Trosdale to abandon his, you will do a capital day's work ; but I think he will carry the furnace into the next world with him. Must you go ?—farewell, then, till our next merry meeting.' And, with a laugh which puzzled

Selwyn, Mr. Ashford bade him once more good-bye.

On the following evening, Stratford's Assistant-Surveyor, as soon as he had closed his office, repaired to East Greenwich and sought out Mr. Matheson, whom he found in a little office that reeked of oil and metal.

'Do I know Mr. Trosdale?' said that gentleman, in answer to his visitor's modest inquiry. 'Well, I did know him once; and I wish to God I never had known him! What's his address? That's more than I can tell you. We did not part on the best of terms; and it's not likely he'd leave it with me. I declare to my Maker I might as well have taken the National Debt on me as that damned thing of his he called a furnace! The money I lost over it! But, there, I needn't bother you. Like a fool, I went in for a profit, and I didn't get one. That is the whole story—and enough for me. The next time I burn my fingers with a patent, call me what you like.'

Which was all Selwyn got by his visit to East Greenwich by way of Lancashire. Perhaps Mr. Ashford had a shrewd idea he would not get much more.

CHAPTER X.

FOUND.

T happened while Selwyn was in Liverpool that an aunt of Mr. Carthew's died, and left him a legacy. Though nothing large, it was sufficient, in conjunction with his pension, to keep him in tolerable comfort, and he at once made up his mind to resign. This determination was hardly a surprise to his Assistant, for he did not think his chief qualified by nature for a post in which well-developed combative powers were essential to success. He was too well-disposed to disbelieve any piteous tale brought to him by a whining knave; and in face of a blustering impostor he could command only a certain mild dignity that was absolutely of no avail.

Selwyn fancied that the letter from the Board, which acknowledged and accepted the resignation, was not very regretful; nor did the Superintending Inspector when he came down to take over the district show more than a decent amount of sorrow at the departure of an old Surveyor. In fact, when Mr. Carthew had shaken hands and left the office for the last time, carrying with him all his office possessions in a shabby black portmanteau, Mr. Tenterden, who was a stranger to Selwyn, remarked:

'I don't mind telling you, Mr. Serle, it's not half a bad thing that Carthew has gone. His work, you know—it wasn't—well, it really was not—*quite* up to the mark! Don't you know what I mean? Oh! he was an awfully good fellow; the kindest man in the world, I dare say; but a shocking old woman!'

'I think you are rather hard on him,' said Selwyn. 'I liked him.'

'Of course you did. Dare say I should too, if I'd been under him, and could have made up my mind to do his work as well as my own.'

Selwyn smiled. It was impossible to deny that he had done this.

'Well, now to business, Mr. Serle. It is not convenient to appoint another Surveyor to this district immediately; and as I am aware that you have had the labour, though not the responsibility of it, for the last few months, I propose to leave it in your charge for the present.'

Selwyn could only say that he was obliged for the confidence Mr. Tenterden reposed in him.

'Yes, of course,' replied that gentleman, twisting his moustache, and regarding Selwyn stonily through his eyeglass; 'great opportunity for you, don't you know? Very sure you'll make a good use of it, however. Glad to have the chance of doing you a service. I always thought Dandison wrong in not pushing the young men forward.'

What would be Mr. Dandison's wrath, Selwyn reflected, if in the midst of his labours in the southern districts he were told that his *locum tenens* had selected to be

'pushed forward' the one young man in the
service whom he looked upon as disgraced?
Selwyn trusted devoutly that no little bird
would fly down to Dorsetshire with the
news; but at the worst it was consoling to
find that his character was not lost with all
the chiefs of his department.

After renewed expressions of confidence,
Mr. Tenterden took his leave, having in his
own estimation done a notable piece of business. In the first place, he had encouraged a
young man, and spurred him on to greater
exertions. In the second, he had provided
for the work of the Stratford district being
done by an Assistant-Surveyor and two clerks,
without any additional assistance, in return
for the loss of Mr. Carthew. That is to say,
he had relieved the department, for the time
at least, of the payment of about £400 a
year, the amount of Mr. Carthew's salary.
Lastly, he had seized the opportunity of turning what Mr. Dandison intended to be to
Selwyn's disadvantage very much to that
young man's profit; and this was, perhaps,
the most pleasing consideration of the three
to Mr. Tenterden.

While this worthy servant of the Board
did what the French call 'his possible' to
apply in all other districts the encouraging
and economical policy which he had conceived, Selwyn was toiling almost day and
night to fulfil punctually the trust reposed in
him. His burden was no light one. The
clerks who had replaced Mr. Murphy and his
hopeful nephew were ignorant of the very rudi-
ments of their work, and had to be trained
even into neatness of handwriting and
orderly arrangement of figures. Fortunately
they were both quiet, steady lads, whilst one
of them showed a real capacity for his duties,
and a disposition to master them. He
speedily became very useful to Selwyn, who
encouraged him with all his power, and gave
up a portion of his scanty leisure to assisting
him to master the Acts of Parliament relating
to Income Tax.

Nothing, however, could very greatly lessen
the amount of work which the Assistant had to
do himself, and of which the severest part
consisted, as usual, in interviewing irate taxpayers. These gentlemen, after their kind,
showed the most irritating want of reason-

ableness. They had grumbled heartily at Mr. Carthew; they were at first absolutely contemptuous of his successor. Sometimes they adopted a sarcastic manner, affecting incredulity when told by Selwyn that he was the Surveyor, and insisting in language of unnecessary plainness that he was imposing on them; sometimes they protested against the conceit of 'a raw, featherless fledgling' in presuming to know more about taxes than they, who had paid them before he was born; sometimes they absolutely refused to accept his decisions, and wrote furious letters to Somerset House, denouncing him and all his works.

Mr. Tenterden, however, rendered Selwyn a loyal support; and after a few weeks had passed, many of the inhabitants of the district began to acknowledge they met with invariable courtesy in the tax-office, even under strong provocation; and that if Selwyn's hand were firmer than his predecessor's, he was also scrupulously just and even forbearing.

It will readily be understood that during this period of hard work Selwyn had no opportunity of continuing his search for the Trosdales ; nor, indeed, if he had been totally unoccupied would he have known in what direction to look. Never, until those dreary weeks, had he understood the ease with which a person may disappear in London ; and while living without appearance of mystery, baffle almost every effort at discovery. Madge and her father seemed to have left no more trace of their movements than a single boat leaves on the ocean after it has passed.

It was useless to look further. Selwyn knew it, and the knowledge added to the bitterness of his regret and self-reproach. It was a miserable time. In everything he thought of or did, the Trosdales entered like two spectres, and were for ever by his side. In his office, where he was hardly more in command than in the old days in Liverpool, he found himself listening for Trosdale's entrance ; when he went home to his dreary lodgings, and sat alone, trying to occupy his mind and to turn it from the bitter thoughts which would present themselves at every moment, the voice of Madge

Trosdale sounded through the room, and he often started round in his chair, expecting fully to see her at his side.

In the end, Selwyn's robust health failed. He slept badly, and began to loathe his meals. He found his head often confused in the daytime, and was once or twice obliged to give up work early in the day, and go out into the fresh air. Mr. Tenterden observed this one day when Selwyn had gone up to Somerset House to consult him about a difficult case.

' You're overdoing it, Serle,' he said. ' Don't break down just now, there's a good fellow! It would be very inconvenient to replace you.'

' I don't think I shall break down,' Selwyn said ; ' but I have a good deal of anxiety at present, and I think if I could take a couple of days' holiday that I should be set up again.'

' Don't see why you shouldn't manage that,' said his chief. ' Why not run down to Brighton for a day or so—or Hastings? I've a little cottage at Hastings. You might go there from Saturday till Tuesday, or something of that sort.'

Selwyn thanked his chief, but declined the offer; he preferred to go to some place on the river—he thought Marlow; and it was arranged that he should come up again towards the end of the week, and if no troublesome business intervened, be granted leave from the following Saturday.

The leave was granted without difficulty; and when Saturday arrived, the Assistant-Surveyor left his office rather early, with the intention of calling at Somerset House on his way to Waterloo.

When he reached Fleet Street, Selwyn, who had eaten no breakfast, began to feel faint for want of food, and, looking at his watch, found that he had time to break his fast before going further. He turned, therefore, into Wine Office Court, that ancient alley in which the 'Old Cheshire Cheese' still shows a bold front to the street-improver, and cheerily defies him and all his sinful doings. The Assistant had frequented this quaint old tavern during many of his brief visits to London; so that its sanded floors, and the almost rustic simplicity of its interior, inspired him with a home-like feeling which always impelled him to return. As he entered the narrow alley in which the ancient 'Cheese' is situated, he brushed past a man who was going towards the street, and who, turning as if to apologize for the awkwardness of his movements, presented to him the well-known features of Mr. Kerry.

Far from appearing pleased to see his friend, the Irishman made a comical face, which he no doubt intended to express contempt, and walked up Fleet Street at the top of his speed. Selwyn, though surprised at this reception, was not to be baffled so easily, and in two or three minutes he had caught Kerry by the arm.

'Kerry, is it you really? I thought you were still in the North. When did you come back? Why didn't you let me know you were in town? Didn't you get my letter?'

'Oh yes! I got it, and put it at the back of the fire,' was the uncourteous reply.

'After you had read it, I hope,' said Selwyn. 'But what does this mean, Kerry? You don't seem glad to see me. Have I vexed you in any way?'

'You have,' replied his friend abruptly.

'I'm mighty angry with you. At least, I'm mistaken in you, and I think we'd both better go our own ways.'

'What on earth do you mean? What cause can you have for anger with me? We were on the best of terms when we parted last year.'

'Ah! but there's a lot of things happened since then.'

'There have indeed; but I don't know of any which accounts for your conduct.'

Mr. Kerry only grunted, and turned round as if to pursue his way.

'Come,' said Selwyn, 'there is some mistake here, Kerry.'

'Devil a mistake!' ejaculated the Irishman.

'Well, some misunderstanding. Call it what you like; but though we have seen nothing of each other for so long, I can't afford to lose a good friend without knowing why, and after all the pleasant hours we passed together you won't refuse to tell me that.'

'I wish you wouldn't be pulling me that way—in the street, too,' said Mr. Kerry peevishly. 'Let go hold of my arm. You know what's the matter as well as I do.'

' I don't indeed.'

' Then I'll tell you. It's ingratitude's the matter, and that's worse than blood-taking, any day. So now, I'll say good-morning, Mr. Serle ; and God send you may mend your ways !'

' Not so fast,' said Selwyn, speaking very seriously ; ' you owe me an explanation now, and you shall give it me. Come across the street, it is quiet in Serjeant's Inn, and tell me what mischievous stories about me you have been listening to. Nay, you must come.'

Mr. Kerry resisted a little, but finally gave way to Selwyn's importunity, and followed him beneath the gateway of Serjeant's Inn.

' Now,' said Selwyn, when they had entered the quiet enclosure, ' here we can talk in peace, and you must kindly tell me in what way I have given you cause to complain of ingratitude.'

' Not me,' replied Mr. Kerry ; ' but where's Trosdale ? Tell me that !'

' Trosdale ! I'd give anything to know ; what have you heard about Trosdale ? Don't

torture me, Kerry ; do you really know anything about him ?'

' More than you'd like me to, or I'm mistaken.'

' For Heaven's sake speak out! I lost
the Trosdales months' ago.   I've searched
London up and down for them ; not a street
in all the Soho and West Central District
that I haven't wandered through for hours
trying to discover them.   They've not returned to Liverpool, they've not been heard
of at Somerset House ; and I'm nearly heart-
broken at not being able to find them.'

There was an evident passion in Selwyn's words, and yet more in the gesture
with which he accompanied them, that impressed Mr. Kerry with their truth.   His
harsh features relaxed a little, and he said in
a more friendly tone :

' Then you haven't heard Trosdale's ill ?'

' Ill, no!   He was well when I saw him
last.   Seriously ill ?'

' Pretty well !' said Mr. Kerry, nodding ;
' just about as bad as living on air makes a
man.'

' And Madge—Miss Trosdale ?'

'She's not the better for starving a little; but she's not much the worse either.'

'Kerry, Kerry! are you trying to madden me?' cried Selwyn. 'What do you mean by starving? Why should they starve? There could be no need for that?'

'Need or not, they nearly did it; and you may think what you like about their doing it from choice.'

'I don't understand you,' said Selwyn angrily. 'I think you are playing some infernal trick with me. Let me tell you, I won't stand jesting on this subject.'

'Faith, it's very far I am from jesting,' said the Irishman; 'and so would you be, Serle, my boy, if you'd been with Trosdale this while past, and listened to him lying on his back chanting, chanting all the time some silly nonsense or other, and him only just pulled back into the world again, like a drowning man, by his hair.'

Then, seeing that Selwyn was very strongly moved, the Irishman laid his hand on his quondam friend's shoulder.

'Maybe I've been hasty with you, and if I have, I'm not the worse for saying so.

But you shouldn't be sharp with a fellow who's had overmuch to torment him. Sure I wonder sometimes is this Dan Kerry that used to be, or some other poor divil with no more heart in him than a sheep going to the butcher !'

' I don't know what you're alluding to in the least,' said Selwyn ; 'but have I had nothing to torture me ? You talk as if you supposed I had neglected the Trosdales, as if I had lost sight of them from choice while I was bent on amusing myself some other way.'

' And if I might make so bold, Mr. Serle,' asked Kerry curiously, ' how did you lose them ?'

' What is that to you ? You take too much on yourself, Kerry, when you question me in such a tone.'

' Sorrow a one of me knows any d———d thing about it all,' answered the Irishman. And with that he set his back against the railings, and pursed up his lips to whistle ; but no sound came, so low-spirited was he.

' Now, will you give me Trosdale's address ? That is the only thing you can do to oblige or help me.'

'And if I didn't want to do either the one or the other,' said Kerry drily; 'how then, my boy?'

'Then I shall follow you, and find out for myself where you go.'

'You'd find that harder than you think. But I'm not going to bother you, Serle. I'm going up there now, and I'll take you with me, if you've time.'

'I was going up to Somerset House to see Tenterden.'

'Then you'll not see him, because I saw him crossing Waterloo Bridge in a mighty hurry half an hour ago, all dressed up in white flannels, as if he was bound for the river.'

Selwyn hesitated a moment, then said:

'Well, give me the address, and I will go now.'

'I didn't say I'd do that,' answered Kerry, with a curious constraint; 'we'll go together.'

'Very well, be it so,' agreed Selwyn; and the two men turned and went out into Fleet Street together.

'If you haven't had any lunch you'd better be having some,' suggested Mr. Kerry, 'because devil a bit you'll get at Trosdale's.'

Selwyn shook his head. His appetite had entirely gone, and the idea of food was hateful to him.

'Then we'll walk up,' said Kerry ; and he turned, crossing Fleet Street northward. Selwyn walked beside him in silence, and for some time each man remained absorbed in his own thoughts.

Kerry led the way through a labyrinth of streets winding in and out, out and in, till they reached the upper part of Gray's Inn Lane. Then he turned up a narrow alley which was unknown to Selwyn, and emerged into a mean court which lay broiling under the midday sun.

'This cannot be very far from Doughty Street,' said Selwyn, breaking silence at last.

'It's not,' replied his friend shortly; and he stopped in front of a little huckster's shop, of which the house-door stood ajar.

'Good God! this is not the place!' exclaimed his companion. 'They cannot possibly live here.'

'Ah, anybody comes down like a lump of lead when all the money's spent. It's hard to know where the bottom is. And now, my good young fellow, listen to me,' he went on. ' You'll just have to shut up your feelings when you get inside, and go about as if you'd been here early this morning, and only gone to get a whiff of ozone, which is what you won't get inside this house.   Trosdale's been mighty ill, and he has no strength to make a song about yet.'

So saying, he led the way to the second story, where he tapped at the door of the front room.   A voice from within bade them enter, and they did so, Kerry first.

It was a poor and miserably furnished apartment, to which some efforts had been made to give a semblance of comfort by means of articles in strange contrast with their surroundings.   A reading-desk stood beside the bed, so arranged that it could be stretched across it at any angle ; and near the window was placed a luxurious easy-chair, in the depths of which, swathed in blankets, lay a gaunt and haggard figure Selwyn could scarcely recognise as that of the ex-Surveyor. An elderly woman in a plain black nurse's dress was in the room, but Selwyn looked in vain for Madge.

Trosdale stirred as they entered, and turned his eyes languidly towards the door.

' I'm glad to see you back, Kerry,' he said feebly, and then closed his eyes again. Selwyn did not speak; had he known the state of weakness to which his former chief was reduced, he would not have risked the excitement of an interview. Making a sign to Kerry, he was about to escape quietly, when Trosdale re-opened his eyes, and said with a wan smile : ' Is it you, Selwyn ? You are very good to come. I have wanted you. I have been ill, you know.' Then he added, trying to raise himself, 'But I am better now.'

' I see you have been very ill, my dear kind friend,' said Selwyn, his voice trembling a little ; ' I should have been here long ago if I had known where to come.'

He put his arm around the old man, and raised him up into the position he was trying to attain. Then Trosdale asked :

' How did you find out ?'

' I met Kerry, and he told me.'

The ex-Surveyor nodded.

' Kerry has been very good,' he said—' the best of friends.'

'Now, Serle, will you not make him talk?' interposed Kerry; 'Mrs. Webber, you interfere, and send this foolish lad away.'

'Indeed, I think it would be better for the gentleman to go now,' said the nurse. 'It is the first time Mr. Trosdale has been up, and he's not very strong yet.'

Selwyn rose to go, but Trosdale held him by the hand.

'You'll come back; you won't stay away so long again,' he said:

'I'll come back every day,' said Selwyn; and with that promise the invalid appeared content, for he released his hold on the young man, and watched him as he left the room with a smile such as had rarely visited his face in the old querulous, anxious days in Liverpool.

Selwyn left the room with a sick feeling at his heart, and an undefined dread of some further shock to come. He had not seen Madge; how was it she was not in her father's room? How had she borne the privations which told so fearfully on the strong man?

He paused irresolutely on the landing,

determined not to leave the house without knowing all, but uncertain where he might wait until Kerry, or Madge herself, should come. The door of the back-room stood partly open, and, seeing that it was empty, he went in, and stood looking out of the window at the prospect beneath. His heart sickened as he gazed upon grimy backyards in which the affectation of a few stunted flowers only rendered their squalor more perceptible; on chimney-pots, broken and hanging, as if they threatened death to some passer-by at any moment when the wind might rise; houses extending as far as he could see without break, obscuring the sky, obstructing any current of air which was not exhausted and robbed of its health-giving properties long before it passed from the green fields and breezy hillsides over such a waste of houses and densely packed humanity as parted them from Battle Bridge.

'What they must have suffered!' he said aloud. 'How much they must have suffered!'

And then he fell into a musing fit, in which his thoughts wandered back to Liverpool and the times when he had first known the Trosdales—not so long ago, though the events of a lifetime seemed crowded into that narrow space ; and when he let his mind recall the house in St. Paul's Square, with its comfortable furniture, quaint and homely, and then turned his eyes on the misery of the room in which he stood, the choking in his throat rose again, and he turned away from the window, and began to pace the room with rapid steps.

Suddenly his heart gave a great leap, for he heard a step on the stair—a step he would have known among a thousand others. In a moment he was out on the landing, and had grasped once more the hand of the only girl he had ever loved. In the same instant the door of the front-room opened, and Kerry came out.

He stood still for a moment, and then advanced towards them, saying :

' I was looking for the both of you ; you're beforehand with me. Come in, Miss Trosdale ; don't be standing there, and you so weak and ill.'

' I am not ill now,' said Madge, with a

weary smile, as she led the way into the back-room.

'For all that you may as well sit down,' observed the Irishman dryly, and there was a tone in his voice which Selwyn had never heard in it before. He placed Madge in a rickety chair, and leaving Selwyn to take the only other seat the room contained, he withdrew to the window, where he stood looking out, as Selwyn had stood a few minutes before.

Selwyn drew his chair towards Miss Trosdale, and laid his hand on hers.

'You look very pale,' he said. 'Your eyes are hollow. Madge, you have been ill, and your father near death. How could you have the heart to hide yourselves from me?'

She withdrew her hand and held it up at him with a pleading expression, from which he comprehended that for some reason she asked him to treat her as if they had never been more than mere friends.

'We have not been so destitute of help as you think,' she said; 'we have had several friends as good as even you could wish. Mr. Kerry has been a host in himself.'

'You let him help you when you would not write to me! What had I done that you should punish me so hardly.'

Madge hesitated, and flushed scarlet; then answered timidly:

'We—we thought you must have left London.'

'That's an unworthy excuse,' said Selwyn hotly. 'I had not left Stratford; and if I had, a letter addressed to Somerset House would have found me at any time.'

Madge was silent, and Kerry remained looking out of the window. Selwyn went on, but less excitedly:

'You have been very cruel to me, Madge.'

She made a deprecatory little movement of the hand.

'Yes, you have. I parted with you in Frith Street, through no fault of my own. I had done no wrong; it was a pure misunderstanding on your father's part, as you well knew. I thought he would come to think differently of the matter; I hoped from day to day to hear from you. Then I found that you had gone, leaving no word for me. Ah, how I searched for you! I think you would have pitied me if you had seen me wandering through the streets till they grew empty and deserted, in the faint hope that I might see you even in the distance. I went down to Liverpool, but you had not been heard of; and it was only in the last few weeks that I gave up the search, and tried to accustom myself to the knowledge that you had cast me off. And now I find you again, ill and in poverty; and it is Kerry who has been with you throughout—Kerry whose privilege it has been to help and to console you. Madge, I had the right to expect better usage from you.'

Kerry turned round quickly.

'It was a mere chance, Serle, that I found out the address.'

'It was a chance which never favoured me,' replied Selwyn gloomily.

Madge was sitting with her hand pressed to her forehead, so that her face was half concealed. She rose now, and the two men could see that she was weeping.

'My father will want me,' she said; 'I have been away a long time.' And then, holding out her hand to Selwyn, she said:

'You should not be hard on me. You have not any cause—not much cause.'

And with these words, spoken in a trembling voice, she left the room. They heard her go into her father's chamber and close the door.

CHAPTER XI.

MR. KERRY EXPLAINS.

MR. KERRY had resumed his former position, but he now turned round and picked up his hat, saying :

' I suppose it's no use staying here any longer.'

' I suppose not,' rejoined Selwyn ; and they went down the stairs, and out into the stuffy court and the narrow street beyond. There Selwyn broke ground.

' This is just a little unsatisfactory. Don't you think so, Kerry ?'

' What's unsatisfactory ?'

' How dense you are ! I want to understand rather more clearly what my own position is, and what yours is too.'

The Irishman did not reply at first, but walked on for some distance with his hands in his trouser-pockets.

'Look here, Serle,' he said at last, 'how many's the time I've told you you're little better than a fool? and sorrow 'fall me if I don't think to-day you're an ill-tempered fool. Maybe you think you're hardly dealt by?'

'I do,' interrupted Selwyn, 'and that by more people than one.'

'Don't be interrupting me. You've been better treated than you've any right to expect; and if you'd only look round, you're as fortunate a fellow as there is in London, and you deserve it less. Now, don't speak! We're going now to my rooms in Guilford Street—a decent place, but too dear for me, if I wasn't obliged to keep up appearances. We'll get a bite of food there, and after we've had that—not before, mind—I'll you all I know about the Trosdales. That's a fair offer; you can take it or leave it.'

'I will come,' said Selwyn. 'I believe you mean me well.'

'You're mighty polite all of a sudden,'

laughed his friend, half bitterly. ' But I do mean you well, my boy, in spite of what you may think. Will we walk or get a cab ?'

' I would rather walk,' answered Selwyn ; ' but just as you like.'

' We'll walk,' decided the Irishman ; ' it's better and it's cheaper.'

Little more was said until they reached Mr. Kerry's apartments. Notwithstanding his swagger on the subject of keeping up appearances, the two rooms which he rented on the second-floor were but shabbily furnished, and ill corresponded to the dignity which their tenant assumed from time to time when he remembered his rise in the world. A slatternly servant-maid answered his ring, and, having received his orders with a nod and a curious glance at the stranger, disappeared into the lower regions. Selwyn went over to the window and looked out.

' It's a good neighbourhood, this,' remarked Kerry, in the tone of a man stating an undoubted fact; ' there's lots of rich people about here. I see them in their carges ' (he always spoke this word as if it consisted of two syllables only), 'each one finer than the last.'

'I don't dislike the street,' replied Selwyn; 'it's healthy, I believe, and well within reach of everything. But I certainly preferred Miss Dormer's rooms in Liverpool.'

'That's because you've no taste for high life. Some people haven't any, and can't get it. Not but what Miss Dormer was a very good sort of woman. I had a letter from her yesterday.'

'And how is she?'

'She's all right, and she says she's coming up to London. I don't know what for, and I wrote and said she'd better stay where she is.'

'Wasn't that a little unsympathetic?'

Mr. Kerry rose, and wound up the clock savagely, muttering beneath his breath that he'd no patience with people who couldn't stay in their own homes.

It was not long before dinner appeared. The meal was despatched in utter silence, and when it was cleared away Mr. Kerry drew an easy chair to the table, and pointed to a second one in which Selwyn might sit.

Then, having filled his pipe, he crossed his legs and said :

'It's like old times, Serle, you and me being together this way. But it's different, because we're not the same ourselves— neither you nor me.'

'I have not changed,' said Selwyn, 'though I've passed through as much trouble in the last twelve months as might have made me old.'

'Trouble !' repeated Mr. Kerry scoffingly ; 'as if nobody else ever had any ! That's the way with all you English ; you're so much wrapped up in yourselves that you never think other people may be in trouble too. I don't care about that, though ; when a man has just been hard hit over the head he doesn't think of calling out about a pin-prick.'

Selwyn gazed at his companion wonder-ingly. He failed altogether to comprehend his meaning.

'Don't be looking at me like that,' said Kerry ; 'sit down and listen to me. I'm going to tell you all I know about the Trosdales.'

He was silent for a few minutes, as if collecting and arranging his ideas; then he began:

'You know very well that when I got my promotion and came up to Somerset House I used to go to Trosdale's place in Frith Street. You gave me the address.'

He looked towards Selwyn for confirmation of this, and the latter nodded.

'I think Trosdale was right glad to have me there. He used to talk about sport, and the fish he caught in his good days in the country, before he began to fiddle away his brains into pap over pots and pans. And Miss Trosdale, bless her! was as glad as the angels in heaven to see someone she knew coming in and out to 'liven her loneliness. I always saw she brightened up when I came in; and well she might, for it wasn't fit for a dog or a tame rabbit, the life she led.'

'Can't you make the story shorter, Kerry?' asked Selwyn, wincing perceptibly at these details.

But Mr. Kerry deigned no reply.

'Two or three days before you came to town,' he went on, 'Tenterden sent for me.

Dandison was away—just started on his journey round the southern districts—and it's hard he's wishing now that he hadn't gone!'

'Why?'

Mr. Kerry took his pipe out of his mouth and sat bolt upright.

'You don't mean to say you haven't heard?'

'Heard what? I've heard nothing.'

'They've shelved him, my boy!' Kerry shouted triumphantly; 'laid him by in lavender on the top shelf, high up.'

'Shelved Dandison! How? What have they made him?'

'A Special Commissioner; and it's little now he'll trouble either you or me in future, unless he has to make a special assessment on one of us; and we'll have to get a good deal more money before that happens. But don't be interrupting me. Tenterden sent for me, as I said, and bid me go to Carlisle at once, for Toomer was ill. Well, I went, and stopped till Toomer got better. Then he had leave to go away, and he got bad again; and, to cut a long story short, he got better and worse, better and worse, till he died. Tenterden was in the North at the time, and came to Carlisle

and asked would I stop on. I told him I didn't
care for the place—that I liked London better
—but he said there was no vacancy near
London, and that if I stayed he would remember it to me. He over-persuaded me,
and I stayed. Well, I had enough work to
make an old man of me, and enough bother
to lay me under the daisy quilt, and very little
thanks for it all ; but I got a London district
at last, praise be, just three months ago ; and
you may be sure the first thing I did was to
try and find the Trosdales.'

'And how did you find them ?'

'I'll tell you if you give me time,' answered
Mr. Kerry. 'Before going further, I should
say that, though I hadn't much leisure for correspondence, I had written to them.'

'Them ?' muttered Selwyn.

'Ay—them—both of them ; put that in
your pipe and smoke it—pretty regularly ;
and I'd have written to you, too, if you'd
thought it worth your while to let a man that
always had liked and stood up for you know
how you were getting on. I took my pen
over and over again for the purpose, but then
I said to myself, "No, Daniel, don't be

cheapening yourself; never push forward where you're not wanted." '

' Upon my soul, Kerry——'

' Never mind that now—you didn't write but the once, and then you said you'd write again and tell me how you were getting on, and you didn't, and that is enough ; and, besides, it is not about you I want to talk at all— it's the Trosdales. As I was saying, I wrote to Miss Trosdale, and though she answered me, I took it into my head she didn't care to correspond ; so I dropped that, and contented myself with sending a letter and a present of one sort and another now and again to the old man. Sometimes he answered and sometimes he let it alone. Once I asked about you, and he said he knew nothing about you —that he never saw you, and never wanted to see you again ; that he bitterly regretted he ever had seen you, and only hoped neither in this world nor the next he'd have the misfortune to set eyes on you more. That was pretty stiff ; and as I couldn't make head or tail of what he meant, I thought I'd write and ask the daughter what the dickens you'd been up to.'

'And what did she say?'

'She said there had been a misunderstanding between her father and you; that she knew you were not in fault, but that she would rather say nothing more about the matter.

'"So best." I thought to myself; for on my conscience I always felt Trosdale would do you more harm than good, and I just laid the whole thing on one side, meaning to fish and find out all about it when I came to London. The next time I wrote to Trosdale it was with a bag of game; but the letter came back to me with "Gone away—left no address" on it, and what became of the game I don't know.'

'Well?' asked the younger man.

'Well! did anybody ever hear the like of you with your wells! It is true enough that many a one says "Well, well," when it never was worse with him.'

'I only want to know——'

'What all the rest of the world wants to know—things that are not over-easy to tell. I needn't say, I suppose, I tried to find the Trosdales, but with no result. Then I asked

Tenterden to get me the address where his pension was sent to.'

'I never thought of that,' remarked Selwyn. 'How stupid of me!'

'It wouldn't have been much good if you had,' observed Mr. Kerry, not without a certain triumph, 'for he had commuted it.'

'What?'

'He had commuted it. He had done just the thing anybody might have been sure he would do. Now you can guess why it is they are living, or rather starving, over a chandler's shop, and haven't got enough to keep soul and body together.'

Selwyn rose and paced the room. 'My God!' he said, 'why did I not know this?'

'It is no use asking your Maker such a foolish question,' retorted Mr. Kerry. 'Sure, I can answer it. You did not know because you had not sense enough to find out, that is why. Now, if you had been writing to me as you ought to have been——'

'I was in such trouble. I could not tell you the trouble I was in.'

'Look here, my lad, you'll never do a day's good if you let trouble get the whip hand of you, and make you forget people that don't forget you. It is sitting down and thinking about themselves that brings all the trouble of this world tumbling on men's heads. Consider Trosdale—did he, ever since you knew him, think of anybody but himself?—and see where all his thinking has landed him. I always thought he was changing you. When you first went to Liverpool it's not five or ten minutes you'd have grudged to write to a friend, no matter how sick or how sorry you were.'

'I am afraid I have been greatly to blame,' said Selwyn humbly.

'I know you have been greatly to blame,' returned Mr. Kerry, 'but I won't be hard on you. From the night I took the shine out of you at Mrs. Gibbs' your visage changed towards me, and it changed worse after I met Miss Trosdale in the street just by chance and she said she'd be glad if I'd come and see her. You were a bit jealous, my boy.'

'I was,' agreed the young man, 'and I am. Haven't I cause to be, when I see the terms you are on with the girl I hoped to marry?'

'If you hoped to marry her, why were you so deucedly sly about the matter? Do you expect a man to know out of his own head what is passing in yours? Girls don't care for lovers that seem ashamed of them.'

'Kerry, how *do* things stand between you and Miss Trosdale?' asked Selwyn, passing over, as immaterial, these strictures on his own conduct.

'I'll tell you if you let me alone—but I won't if you keep interrupting me. It's not good manners, and it's not good sense; and want of sense is want of manners. When I heard that about the pension I was stumped. He might have gone to Jerusalem or America, you see. But I had still a notion he had not left London, and I was considering how I'd ferret him out, when one day, as I was taking a short cut up to Pancras Station, who should I see on the other side of the road but Trosdale, looking like a ghost. "Hallo!" says I, "what's happened to him—is he come out to buy a winding-sheet? for it's that he'll soon want." But before I could get up to him he was gone, and for the life of me I couldn't find out where.'

'Why do you stop?' said Selwyn impatiently.

'Do be quiet,' entreated his host. 'I can't rattle out words as fast as you—thank the Lord. Well, I worried myself all that day and the next about Trosdale, thinking maybe it wasn't him after all, but only a spectre, and puzzling over what it could mean, whether it was myself that was going to meet with a disaster, till at long and at last one morning, when I was talking to old Cobbles, the tax-collector, I says:

'" Maybe you don't know anybody called Trosdale in your parish?" just at a venture.

'" Trosdale?" says he. " You mean Trowbridge!"

'" I don't," says I, "and if I had I'd have said it."

'" Trosdale?" says he again, and a kind of light came into his bloated, sinful old face. " Did he live in Liverpool ever?" he asked.

'" You're right now," says I.

'" Why, I've got a certificate of removal against him in my pocket." And with that he pulls out a certificate for thirty-three and ninepence, Inhabited House Duty for the old place in St. Paul's Square. "Devil a rap I can get out of him," says he.

'"Not likely," says I; "I'm his banker." So I paid him the thirty-three and ninepence and took the receipt up that day.'

'That was kind—that was very good of you,' exclaimed Selwyn eagerly. 'But you will——'

'Well? Speak out, man.'

Selwyn hesitated.

'No, I won't,' he said. 'Go on with your story.'

Kerry regarded his friend with a curious look of inquiry, and something like a frown on his forehead; then he proceeded:

'I went up at once; but when I saw what like the place was, I was nearly turning me round and going back. "It's not likely they're here," says I to myself. "Why, the stair is as dirty as if the dust-carts had only just come down it." You never saw such a place, Serle, in all your days—it's been cleaned up since then. When I got up to the landing I felt as sick as a dog, and very near heart-broken to think what Trosdale had brought his daughter to with his d——d folly.

'Well, Miss Trosdale came and opened the door in answer to my knock. I'm glad you didn't see her then, because she looked as if she wasn't long for this world. She's a lot better now, and yet I dare say you didn't think much of her appearance. Will you sit quiet, and not be worrying me by rampaging about that way?'

To sit quiet was the one thing which Selwyn found it impossible to do. Kerry, whether consciously or not, was torturing him by his fulness of detail. He got up, and walked first to the fireplace, then to the window, then threw himself again into his seat, but moved restlessly from side to side as if undergoing irritation which was stronger than his nerves were capable of enduring.

'There were just three chairs in the room,' continued Kerry, 'and a little table, with her Bible on it, and a bed in the corner where you saw it, and Trosdale lying on his back; but he no sooner saw me than he jumped up, and was for trying to get out of bed, so I went at him and held him down; but he was like three men for a while until the fit passed off him. " I'm thankful you've come, Mr. Kerry," says the daughter, when he began to be quiet ; "he's too strong for me, and I don't know what to do." And indeed she didn't, poor girl ; for she was crying as she talked, and " Where's Serle ?" says I ; but I'd much better have held my tongue, for Trosdale was up again like a shot. " Show him me !" he shouted. " Show me the d——d villain !" And then I had the devil's own trouble with him.'

' I can't stand any more of this, Kerry,' Selwyn said, rising up with his hand to his forehead. ' I'm not well—everything seems spinning round. I must get out into the air.'

' Lord save us, are you ill too ?' cried the Irishman. ' I believe you are, my boy ; why didn't you stop me ? God forgive me for thinking you were only cross. There, now, you've got your hat on ; lean on me, and mind that turn in the stairs. Stand steady, man, it isn't waltzing we're after.'

In the fresh night air Selwyn very quickly revived. Kerry took him down through Clement's Inn and Essex Street to the Embankment ; and there they stood for some time leaning over the parapet without speaking. Selwyn took his hat off, and the cool breezes from the lower reaches of the river playing round his temples refreshed and strengthened him. Then he told his former friend that his health had been giving way, and that he had intended that afternoon to go out of town for some much-needed rest. Kerry did not say much; but it was felt by both that in some way the mutual distrust was giving way, and the old confidence gaining ground.

'I think I shall walk home,' said Selwyn, raising himself from the stone balustrade after a period of silence.

'Walk home! Walk to Bow!'

'Well, and why not? It's not more than three miles and a half from here, and I feel the exercise will do me good.'

'I'll come a piece of the way with you,' said his friend; and after a faint protest Selwyn accepted the offer, for which, in truth, he was grateful. They fell into a quick walk, and as they passed Queen Victoria Street towards Aldgate, Kerry told how he had stayed with the Trosdales almost continually for a week after he had found them, sitting up at night and tending the sick man, until he had found a capable nurse to whom he could hand over his charge. And as he listened to the clumsy, awkward sentences in which Kerry related the efforts he had made to provide everything which he thought necessary for Trosdale's comfort, or conducive to his recovery, his friend could not but feel that he had never half appreciated the man.

There was a certain restraint and embarrassment in Mr. Kerry's manner, however, which Selwyn could not wholly account for. He puzzled himself continually about it as they walked together; it was as if Kerry were trying to conceal something from him, as if he wished to lead away the young man's thoughts from some particular phase of the subject they were discussing.

' I do not know how to thank you, Kerry, for all you've done. And I want to tell you that I'm sorry I spoke to you as I did. I am not quite myself; you must try to make excuses for me.'

' It's very likely,' said Kerry, after a short interval of silence, ' that we've both been blind. I know I've been a d——d ass, but

I see it all now. I believe I did all along; but I wouldn't say so to myself.'

Selwyn wondered what he meant by this; but his head was still too confused to comprehend.

'So that's settled, I suppose,' Kerry went on, 'and we're good friends again?'

'The best of friends,' Selwyn answered.

At that moment a clock somewhere in the neighbourhood struck eleven.

'I'm going to leave you now,' said Kerry. 'We've a lot still to talk about, but you'll be the better of a quiet walk; and, besides, I said I'd look in rather late to-night and hear how the doctor found Trosdale. But before we part there's one thing I want to tell you.'

'I can guess it,' answered Selwyn. 'I have expected it all along. You are engaged to Miss Trosdale. Well, I can't blame either of you.'

'You're too clever by half,' said Mr. Kerry banteringly; 'and you'd have no cause to blame either of us if we were engaged, which we are not—through no fault of mine, though. I asked her to marry me. I'll walk on a step with you, and tell you how it came about.

It's easy enough for a man to hide from his friends, or a girl from her lover, but it's hard to find a place a creditor won't forage out. When Trosdale left Liverpool he had some debts, and you may be sure he didn't pay them off while he was dry-nursing that accursed furnace in London. More than that, he got into debt here, and as the people became troublesome, he just shifted his quarters to get rid of them—only he didn't get rid of them; and at last they followed him even to the hole where he is now. One day as I was going in I heard a fellow bully-ragging Miss Trosdale at the length of his tongue. She was telling him she'd pay when her father got his pension ; and one thing led on to another till he got just a bit too impudent, and I pushed open the door, and asked would he go downstairs peaceably or would he wait till I put him down. So then we went at it for a minute or two, and I swore if he didn't clear out I would give him in charge. Miss Trosdale was frightened. She had never seen any row of the sort before, and when I got shut of him she sat trembling, and said—

' "Aren't people dreadful, Mr. Kerry ?"

' "They're divils," I made answer, and then she fell to laughing, and couldn't stop herself; but I was glad to see her doing even that same, for sure laughing is better than crying any day.'

' Go on,' entreated Selwyn.

' Well, when she came a little to, she began talking about the pension, and wondering why it did not come.

' "Can you imagine why they do not send it ?" she asked.

' " I am afraid I can," I answered, and so then I told her straight out what her father had done, for there was no good in letting her make promises she never could fulfil.

' " Taken a lump sum," she repeated after me.

' " And spent it—at least, that is my opinion," I said.

' "Then we have nothing," she cried.

' "I am afraid that's about it."

' Poor thing ! she seemed like one out of her mind. What were they to do ?—their money gone, their furniture gone, their house gone, their connection gone. " I have a few

pupils here," she said, " or at least I had some
till I was taken ill, that I taught at sixpence
and a shilling an hour." Just think of it, and
she but a slip of a girl !' Mr. Kerry did not
speak for a minute, then he began again :

'After that she went on to wonder how
she would ever pay me all I'd lent them, and
I could not stop her, for she was thinking out
loud, poor thing ; and I let her say her say
for a while before I told her she had no cause
to trouble herself about the money. " If it
were fifty times as much, and I had it, your
father would be welcome to every penny ;
but there is one thing I wish you could
do——"

' " What is it ?" she asked ; " only tell
me."

' " It's only to marry me, and put an end
to all your bothers," I said. " I've enough to
keep you in comfort, and I'll be better every
year, and I'll be a loving husband to you and
a good son to your father ; and, for the rest,
I've been fond of you ever since my eyes first
rested on you, and I never did care for any
girl before, except in the way of diversion.
Don't answer me now, but think it over ; and

if you feel you can put up with a fellow that worships the ground you walk on, we'll make a match of it whenever you like."'

'And she?'—Selwyn could not say any more. It cost him an effort even to say that.

'She let me down as easy as she could. She liked me, she said, she never thought to meet with such a friend, she would never forget me, and all the rest—oh! you know.'

'How should I know?' asked Selwyn.

'At any rate, you might know the upshot of it all was she couldn't marry me.

'"Then there is some other fellow?" I said.

'"Yes; but he could never be anything to her." Then it all came upon me with a flash.

'"Is it Serle?" I asked; and with that she confessed it, and that she and you had been engaged.

'"Why isn't he here then?"—I was very plain, you see.

'"He does not know where we are."

'"Then it is his business to know where you are," I answered.'

'So it was—so it was,' commented Selwyn.

' " And if he did know, my father has for bidden him the house."

' " Faith ! and if I was engaged to you, I'd like to see the father who could keep me from you. Now I know who it is, I am not in the least daunted ; but I won't trouble you for the present, or speak again at all till I see some sign." You couldn't find fault with me for saying that.'

' And have you ever seen any sign ?'

' You'd best ask me no more. If you do, I'll not answer you.'

And, without any more ceremonious leave-taking, Mr. Kerry turned on his heel, hailed a passing omnibus, and made his way as fast as the tired horses could take him to Gray's Inn Lane.

CHAPTER XII.

'WHAT CAN THE MATTER BE?'

NATURALLY, though he thought he should not be able to close his eyes, Selwyn slept soundly till nine o'clock the next morning. It was the sleep of utter mental and physical exhaustion. Nevertheless, he awoke from it refreshed, and with a feeling of peace to which he had long been a stranger. At last, Madge was found. Miserable as her position was, uncertain as Selwyn felt about the future, however things might be between them— she was found! The long suspense was ended, the heart-wearying search over. For good or for ill, they had met once again, and, whether her heart remained unchanged or her affection had grown colder, he should now know the best or the worst.

How quickly the events that change the whole course of our lives occur! Since the previous morning Selwyn felt as if he had passed through a whole existence. As he dressed he wondered if he were the same man, and when he looked in the glass, it almost surprised him to see that no outward change had passed over his appearance to render him unrecognisable.

' I will not see Kerry again till I have had an explanation with Madge,' he decided ; ' but I must not disturb my poor girl too early. I will not go there very early—not till after church. I dare say she will go to church.'

Ah ! he did not yet understand, spite of all Mr. Kerry had said, the whole of their poverty. Poor Madge! poor proud Madge! who managed to hide many things even from the inquiring eyes of her Irish admirer.

Perhaps it was some sort of idea that at the same time they would be engaged in the same service, and so be near in spirit though apart in body, which determined

Selwyn. restless as he was, to go to church.

Through all his unhappiness the same fancy had possessed him, and even on that morning he found a vague sort of comfort in turning, on his way west, into St. Swithin's, Cannon Street, where the clergyman told them much about those cares and trials all have to endure, and of which one at least of the congregation thought he had been assigned more than his full share. Then when the service was over he bent his steps towards Mr. Trosdale's latest home, his heart fainting a little as he did so.

Madge passed a miserable night. The meeting of which she had thought and dreamt, for which she had hoped and feared, was over, and Selwyn had left her bitterly dissatisfied. Was that dissatisfaction deserved? This question she repeated to herself through every hour of the endless night, and when morning came it still remained unanswered.

Had she been unkind to him, to the true friend who brought her all the happiness she had known for many a day, and who asked only to share her troubles with her; to the boy-lover who, in his devotion, would have taken all the burdens of her life gladly on his own shoulders, and never complained, however the weight of them might have galled? Not willingly, she answered; for even for him she could not leave her father desolate. She must be bound by his wrath; she could not follow him, and yet step across the breach which he had made with Selwyn.

But, even in spite of her father's injunctions, might she not have written? Why had she not? To this question the answer was less plain. It was not her parent's command, at least not wholly, which restrained her, for in this she held him to be irrational. It was by pride, rather, and shame that she was withheld—pride which made it as impossible for her as for her father to ask an alms; shame which whispered hourly in her ear that it would be wicked to burden Selwyn's young life with the future of two persons on whom the sun of prosperity had never yet shone. Better for him, the warning voice whispered, a thousand times better, that he had never come to Liverpool, never entered

St. Paul's Square. Who had told him that oftener than Madge Trosdale, or meant it more sincerely ? Then why try to patch up the links which had been so painfully broken? Why recall him when the wounds in his heart must be beginning to heal, perhaps had healed ?

Painfully inadequate to justify her silence these arguments appeared to Madge in the retrospect. Yet she believed she had done rightly, and she knew that she had done unselfishly ; for there was no hour since that in which Selwyn closed the door of Frith Street for the last time behind him when her heart had not leaped up with a sudden joy at the sound of a distant footstep coming nearer, to sink again with a mixture of sadness and relief when she found the step was not his.

If she had known with what heart-sick weariness Selwyn was searching for her, her resolution might have given way. Such a proof of tenderness on his part would have conquered her pride ; but the vastness of London separated her from him as effectually as a continent, and of his loving search she knew nothing.   On the other hand, the slender stock of money which was still in her father's hands disappeared with frightful rapidity ; all the employment she could obtain was very scanty; and as her own health began to suffer from privation she was not able to work so much or so well.

All these things strengthened her resolution, and there was nothing to shake it. Now, however, everything was changed. She had taken help from Kerry, she had broken down her pride, but all to no purpose.

And so she tormented herself, going over point by point what had passed, and seeing many things which she ought to have seen, and more than one way in which she might have controlled circumstances instead of yielding to them.   She rose very early, in order to relieve the nurse, and sat by her father through all the morning, listening to the bells ringing for service, and wondering if she should ever see the old church in St. Paul's Square again.   How dusty it was always in the organ loft !   There was one key which had lost its ivory long before she ever touched the instrument.   Had anyone replaced it, she wondered ; did anyone play on the organ who loved it as much as she ?

At one o'clock the nurse relieved her, and Madge went into the back-room, and for very weariness, resting her tired head on the table, fell asleep. Her slumbers were very troubled, dream images being strangely mixed with real appearances, so that when she was suddenly awakened she hardly knew whose arms were round her, whose voice was calling her name.

' Madge, my only love—don't be frightened. It is I, your own Selwyn. My poor darling, forgive me for startling you, but you looked so worn and lonely I could not help taking you to my heart, which has been empty— empty for want of you. Oh ! my love, let nothing and no one come between us any more for ever. Your father was glad to see me yesterday ; he was like his old self again, though so weak and ill. Say you are glad too, dearest ; I have been so miserable.'

She sat back in her chair, and, pushing her hair out of her eyes that still were dazed and heavy with sleep, looked at Selwyn as if trying to remember something; then, as full recollection came back, she unclasped his encircling arms, pushed his face, which was brushing hers, gently away, and gazed steadily at him as she asked :

'Why have you come here?'

'Because I cannot live without you.'

'You lived without me for nearly a year, and it was best so.'

'It was not best so, and I did not live without you of my own will,' he returned. 'When a man loves as I do, every moment of separation seems an age. My love, why will you be so cruel to me? If I spoke sharply yesterday it was only because I felt hurt to see another where I, and I alone, ought to have stood ; but I never could be really angry with you, dear. Kiss me, darling! Let me feel your sweet lips on mine, and know you are as fond of me as you were on that evil night when so much misery fell upon us.'

He stopped, but she made no sign ; instead, with one thin hand, she still kept him from coming closer to her. 'I cannot speak yet,' she said ; 'wait a little.'

Something in her manner, something in

her face, filled him with a terrible apprehension.

'What is it, my Madge?' he asked. 'Whatever it is, let me know at once—anything is better than suspense. Have you ceased to care for me—is it that?'

She shook her head.

'Have you found anyone you care for more?'

For answer she smiled—but it was a wan, sad smile.

'Madge, you will drive me mad,' he said. 'Tell me what it is that has come between us at once—I have a right to know—I insist on knowing. We are not children, that we should play at puzzles; I for one don't like them. Remember, our whole future is hanging in the balance now, the happiness of our lives is at stake. If you love me, say so; if I have offended you, say so; if you have bound yourself to any other person, say so. I don't mean to vex you, my poor, tried darling, but do strive and realize what this silence means to me.'

She looked up at him, her lovely eyes full of tender sorrow.

'I did not think I should ever see you again,' she said with a pitiful appeal.

'Are you grieved to see me?'

'For your sake, yes——'

'Never mind about my sake,' he returned. 'I must decide about my own future. I am the best judge of what will be happiest for me. Don't let us go over all that old ground again, which we traversed so often before we knew how much we should come to be to each other. For your sake, are you grieved to see me? That is the only important question now; are you? Oh, my love! my dear love——' and casting himself on the ground, he seized her hand and laid his cheek upon it.

She did not withdraw her hand, but she turned her head away to hide the tears that were blinding her.

'If I have vexed you, forgive me,' he went on; 'if I seemed somewhat hard yesterday, think what it must have been to know you had needed me, and yet would not write one word which would have brought me to you instantly. Oh, Madge! it is you who were hard to me; don't add to the wrong. Not a day, not an hour, not a minute, since we parted, but you have been in my thoughts. Man was never more faithful to woman than I to you. Won't you speak to me? Won't you tell me what has come between us, my love? How am I to unloosen your tongue? How can you hear me plead and remain dumb?'

'I want——' she began.

'Yes, dear——'

'I want you to do something for me.'

'I will do anything for you, providing it be not to leave you.'

'It is to leave me for a while. I want you to go away now, and send Mr. Kerry here.'

'And when may I come back?'

'I cannot say; I do not know.'

There was a minute's silence; probably that was the hardest minute Selwyn had ever fought through.

He had risen to his feet, and stood looking down at the girl with grave concern, the while a tumult of feelings warred within him.

'I will do your bidding,' he said at last, and without another word went.

As he passed through the door she cried in a half-whisper, 'Selwyn,' but if he heard her he took no notice.

There was but one clear task before him, and he was going to perform it.

Looking neither to right nor left, noticing none of the people he met, scarcely conscious of the streets he passed through, the young fellow walked at the top of his speed to Mr. Kerry's lodgings, where he found that gentleman lying full length on a sofa reading 'The Three Musketeers.'

As Selwyn entered, the Surveyor lazily turned his head and exclaimed :

'Serle, by all the powers ! Where do you think you have come from ?'

'I have come straight from the Trosdales.'

'You have—have you ? Well, and how's the old man ?'

'I don't know ; I did not ask ; I forgot.'

'How's the daughter, then ?'

'I did not ask that either. She wants to see you.'

'What does she want with me ?'

'She did not say.'

'This beats Banagher. Must I go now?'

'You can please yourself, I suppose.'

'And what are you going to do?'

'Stay here till you come back.'

'Oh! that's the way of it, is it?'

'Yes, that is precisely the way of it.'

'You are a bit put out in your temper, aren't you?'

'I am a great deal put out.'

'Well, you're a——'

Selwyn could not exactly catch what he was supposed to be, as Mr. Kerry, rising from his recumbent position, mumbled his opinion of him while moving about the room in quest of various articles of attire he had, for greater ease, cast aside while pursuing his studies.

The Surveyor's toilet was not a lengthy affair. After adjusting his collar, tying his cravat, and slipping on his coat, he looked at himself in the glass; and saying, 'I think I'll do now,' took his hat and moved towards the door.

There he paused for a moment irresolute; but then, with a friendly caution to Selwyn, not to be 'getting into any mischief,' departed.

CHAPTER XIII.

A LITTLE ACCIDENT.

MR. KERRY found Madge in the small room where Selwyn had left her.

'You sent for me?' he said, without any formal preamble.

'Yes. Thank you for coming so soon.'

'That's nothing,' said Mr. Kerry. 'I would do more than that for you any time. How's your father?'

'He is better, I think. He had a fairly good night.'

'Has the doctor seen him to-day?'

'Yes. He says he is stronger on the whole.'

'None the worse for seeing Serle?'

'No.'

There ensued a pause, which was broken by the Surveyor, who asked :

'Now, what is it ?'

'Will you not sit down ?'

'No, thank you ; I'd rather stand.'

And Mr. Kerry again took up his position by the window which commanded so fine a prospect of back-yards.

Madge got up, and crossed over to the window also. It was but a few steps, yet she walked as though setting out on some long journey. When she was within a pace or two of the visitor she stopped, and looked at Mr. Kerry, who in his turn regarded her with a singular expression on his shrewd, plain face.

'I want to tell you something,' she began.

'Do you think I don't know it ?'

'I do not think you do.'

'Then let us hear it,' he remarked.

'Yesterday morning — yesterday morning——' said Madge ; and then she stopped.

'Will I help you ?' he asked.

'No ; I do not want any help. I should like to tell you myself, in my own way.'

' Just as you like,' said the Surveyor ; while his look of curious comprehension never changed.

' You remember what you asked me long ago ?'

' I do, well—to marry me, you mean ?'

' And when I said no, you told me you would not ask me again, unless——'

' Until I saw some sign you had thought better of the matter,' finished Mr. Kerry.

' Have you ever seen such a sign ?'

' I can't say I have ; though once or twice——'

' Yes ; that is what I mean—that is what I want to tell you.   Oh, Mr. Kerry ! we cannot always go on taking, and give nothing back ; and yesterday morning I had made up my mind if you asked me again I would say yes.'

' The deuce you had !'

' Yes ; I felt it would be only right.'

' And now you feel it would be only wrong ?'

' Your kindness, your goodness, have not changed since yesterday morning ; and if you still wish—if I lead you to think——' she stopped and then added, ' that is what I wanted to say.'

'Now, look here,' answered Mr. Kerry, 'let one word serve between us. If you had said all this forty-eight hours ago, I can't tell what I might have done; but I know what I am going to do now. I wouldn't marry you if you were as rich as the Queen of Sheba; I wouldn't marry you if you were Victoria by the grace of God herself, whose servant I am. What, you poor white, innocent lamb! do you suppose I thought to buy you, body and soul, with a few pounds of grapes and pints of turtle? that while I was sitting by listening to your father's maunderings, I was planning how I could best put a knife to the throat of his daughter's happiness? I may be a very poor sort of fellow; but I am not so poor as to marry a girl who has not as much love for me as would cover a fourpenny-bit. If that is what you have been breaking your heart about, make your mind quite easy. You owe me nothing—nothing at all—and if you did, I would not let you pay me this way.'

'You are so good! oh, you are *so* good! I don't know what to say to you,' and Madge laid her hand on the Irishman's shoulder with a thankful gesture which to an outsider would have seemed infinitely touching.

It appeared to affect Mr. Kerry differently, however; for he removed her hand and held it in his own, while his face became drawn with a strained look of pain.

'Say nothing,' he answered. 'There's nothing to say.'

'Indeed there is nothing I can say,' she returned softly; and she laid her other hand on his arm, and she raised her eyes, which were full of gratitude, to his.

Just for a moment he kept silence, then, taking both hands in his and holding them as if in a vice, he said, in a voice that sounded harsh by reason of the constraint he was putting on himself:

'I'd have you remember one thing—a man's a man, and a woman's a woman; and you can't change a man into a woman, work it how you will. If the Almighty had meant him to be one, He would have made him a woman, do you see. No, you don't—well, I'll tell you. When one woman's pleased with another, she kisses her, and there is no harm done; but how would you like me to take you in my arms and kiss you? I have had much striving to help it, yet I would not do such a thing for all the wide world. You are going to marry Serle, and you shan't feel any shame or sorrow about me when you look back if I can keep one or the other from you. I am going to be a father to you, and I'll not let you do anything you ought not. Those soft pretty ways are just destruction—you mean little by them, but they mean a great deal to us, so no more. And I'll send that Othello of a Serle to you, and God bless, and good-bye; but I'll be in again to-morrow to see how your other father is, and you can just forget anything I ever said to you that you had rather not remember, and that it is as well should not be remembered'—having finished which speech, Mr. Kerry released the girl's hand, took his hat, and ran down the stairs as lightly as he could.

'It's you she wants now,' was the only remark he made to Selwyn, whom he found impatiently awaiting his return. 'Such going and coming! I am fairly sick of it. Don't be bringing any more messages to me, I tell you, for the devil another step I'll stir to-day —no, not if the Secretary himself sent for me. It is about time you took your turn' and the Surveyor threw himself on the sofa, and resumed his study of M. Dumas' great work.

Somehow his reading did not quiet him so much as might have been expected—the love passages contained no balm to soothe his own pain; and he was about to close the book and go out for a stroll, when Selwyn reappeared radiant.

'Kerry, my dear Kerry!' he began.

'What's wrong now?' asked Mr. Kerry.

'There is nothing wrong,' answered Selwyn. 'I'm the happiest fellow alive, and it is you who have made me so. How can I ever be grateful enough to you?'

'Bad luck to you, Serle! You're the greatest plague ever I came across—why can't you go on with your courting, and let me alone? Sure this is the only day I have to myself in the week. I am bothered enough with taxes while I am at work, without being bothered with you and your girl when I am at play. Just take yourself off, please, and let me alone. I've other things to think of than marrying and giving in marriage, and so will you before you're much older.'

'I am sorry I disturbed you,' answered Selwyn, a good deal abashed; 'but I could not stay away. Shake hands with me before I go—do, there's a good fellow!'

'I'll shake hands with you: but you're just a heartbreak,' returned Mr. Kerry. And having gone through the desired ceremony with the worst possible grace, he turned round on his side and became again absorbed in his book, leaving Selwyn remorsefully to consider that he might well have deferred speaking either of his raptures or his gratitude to the disappointed swain.

As the evening waxed late, however, Mr. Kerry, who by that time had smoked several pipes and imbibed the contents of three stiff tumblers, began to take a more philosophical view of the situation. He always inclined to think those grapes sour which hung beyond his reach, and though he would have married Madge in spite of all obstacles, if she would only have married him, there was no denying that, even to her, there were objections.

'Maybe it's just as well,' he said to himself, mixing what Mr. M'Closky would have called an 'eke.' 'There was many a

hindrance when I come to think of them.
First I misdoubt she'd never have gone to
mass with me, though, to be sure, I don't go
often ; and I'm afraid it wouldn't have been
just right for me to go with her to the Pro-
testant church. I can't see how we should
have settled it, and I'm glad there is no need
to addle my head about the matter now. Then
old Trosdale's a divil if ever there was one,
and what I'd have done with him dodging up
and down the country after me, needing to
be fed, and clothed, and lodged, and nursed,
most likely keeping me out of my warm bed
when he was ill, and knocking up some
d——d contrivance he'd have been wanting
to waste money on when he was well, the
Lord alone knows. Dan Kerry, there's a
Providence watches over you, and keeps you
out of harm, even when you don't want to
be kept out, but would rather be in the thick
of it. That is good whisky ; maybe the
wife wouldn't have liked you to drink more
than a sup of punch out of a wine-glass.
Phooh ! Cheer up, old boy, you're in favour
with the saints.'

As the liquor in his tumbler diminished,

however, this delightful reflection did not seem to give him quite the comfort it might have been expected to afford. A scowl settled down on his face, and he kicked his heels viciously against the floor, to the great annoyance of a nervous gentleman who occupied the drawing-rooms.

' I wonder which one of the saints it was served me this dirty trick,' he muttered. ' If I knew, deuce a candle, or a picture-card, or any mortal thing else would he get out of me this month of Sundays. But there! what's the good ? I'll go to bed !'

Having arrived at which determination he finished his grog at a draught, turned off the gas carefully, and groped his way out of the room. When he reached the door he recollected that he had left his purse on the chimney-piece, and went back for it. As he did so he tripped over a footstool which ' stood quite convenient for a man-trap,' and, pitching heavily forward, inflicted such injuries on himself that the doctor, who was summoned in hot haste, looked very grave after ending his examination, and said :

' This is likely to be a long business, Mr.

Kerry. Have you any mother or sister in London who could come to nurse you ?'

'I have nobody in London,' answered the Surveyor faintly; 'but there is "one" in Liverpool would come fast enough if she was asked.'

'I will ask her then,' replied the doctor; and he at once sat down and wrote a note to Miss Dormer, telling her exactly what had happened, and begging her to come to town without delay. The result of which appeal was, that when the temporary nurse, sent in to attend to the patient, was fairly at her wits' end, and Mr. Kerry in the highest state of fever and irritability, the telegraph boy brought this soothing message :

From	*To*
Miss Dormer,	Daniel Kerry, Esq.,
0A, Duke Street,	1909, Guilford Street,
Liverpool.	London, W.C.

'So shocked and grieved ; coming by next train.'

'When's that ?' grumbled Mr. Kerry. 'Sure, she might have said the time.' But he grew quieter afterwards, and actually fell asleep.

Miss Dormer's heart was very full of love and pity for Mr. Kerry; but, though she lost no time in obeying the doctor's summons, she felt it due to her position as a gentlewoman not to allow sentiment to gain such an ascendancy as to induce her to appear before her quondam lodger's delighted eyes in any except the finest war-paint her wardrobe could furnish.

'Men are so apt to cast those sort of things up at one afterwards,' she considered, as the train whizzed past Harrow. 'They forget the moving circumstance, and only remember a lady's appearance;' for which reason, ere going to Guilford Street, she drove to an hotel near King's Cross, where her ever-to-be-revered papa had been in the habit of resorting, and there, figuratively, put herself in dry dock for repairs.

When she again presented herself before the gaze of the public, she was indeed something worth looking at. She might have been one of that remarkable sisterhood who, in former days, were twice a year to be seen journeying to the Bank of England for their six months' annuity. Such a band of old ladies, dressed in such clothes, will never again be beheld in the London streets. It was a pity Government did away with that show.

'A bonny bride is soon buskit,' says the Scotch proverb: but Miss Dormer was neither a bride nor very bonny, and though her toilet occupied a considerable time, the result was by no means commensurate with the labour bestowed.

'What do you come here dressed like that for?' asked Mr. Kerry, when, the first greetings over, he devoted himself to the contemplation of his nurse's person. 'The gown you've on was your grandmother's, wasn't it? A beautiful silk—is that what you say?— would stand alone? I don't care. Take it off, and put on something reasonable, which won't make a noise or cause you to look like a great-grandmother yourself. Where's that pretty brown thing you wore the night I got my promotion? Sure, that is far and away better than those old clothes of people long dead and gone.'

But Miss Dormer, whose sense of decorum was very great, refused, for the first evening at least, to appear in any light and skittish attire.

'I am very glad to be able to come,' she explained—'thankful to know I shall be of any use; but I feel I cannot be too careful.'

'Careful about what?' asked Mr. Kerry. Then, before she could answer, he added diplomatically, 'Hand me some of that lemonade, will you, like a good soul; my tongue is just cleaving to the roof of my mouth. Thank you. I feel better already for the sight of you. There are no friends like old friends, after all.'

'I suppose you have made a great many new ones since you left Liverpool?' hazarded Miss Dormer, a little wistfully.

'Scores on scores,' was the answer. 'Sure, I told you so when I ran down at Christmas. A man can't go here and there about the world and keep himself the same as a hermit. And now I think I'll rest myself for awhile; I feel tired.'

Mr. Kerry was indeed so tired, that when the doctor came in the evening he said he must be kept very quiet, and not allowed to see anyone or to excite himself in any way; and somehow the idea crept through the house that the Surveyor was in a very bad state, which was the news that met Selwyn when, on the Tuesday evening, he looked in before proceeding to the Trosdales'. He had relinquished the week's leave granted to him, which was quite as well, since, when he went to the office, he found a pile of troublesome work lying there, at which the gentleman sent down to take temporary charge was sitting looking in utter dismay.

'I'll see to all that,' said Selwyn cheerfully. In good truth happiness made him strong enough even to kill dragons, and accordingly he went in among the tax difficulties, and, laying ruthlessly about him to right and left, he soon found himself with a pile of slain around.

But he could not spare time to go up west till Tuesday evening, when, as a sort of salve to his conscience, which could not feel quite easy about his friend, he took the Irishman's lodgings in a round-about route to the Trosdales'.

'So you have not heard, sir,' said the servant who answered the door, and who was

the same he had seen on the previous Saturday. (How far, far back in the remote past
that Saturday seemed!) 'Poor Mr. Kerry!
He has fractured his arm and broken two of
his ribs, and got a great cut on his head ; and
he's out of his mind, and the lady and the nurse
were up with him the whole of the night, and
the doctor says he's bad as bad can be ;' and,
though full, of course, of sympathy, the girl
looked immensely pleased to see the effect
of her evil tidings on Mr. Kerry's friend.
It only needed one more touch to render
that effect complete, and quite unconsciously
the damsel gave it:

'And the poor lady she has been a-crying
so.'

'This is deadful!' exclaimed Selwyn.

'The doctor told her not to take on ; only
he said Mr. Kerry must keep himself quiet.'

'Yes, of course,' thought Selwyn bitterly ;
but would he ever keep himself quiet where
Madge was ? And what right had she, a
girl, to be there at all—she, Selwyn's
affianced wife—she, the woman Kerry had
wished to marry ? He could hardly contain
himself ; he could not even feign grief for

Mr. Kerry's accident. The demon of jealousy was strong within him at that moment—it had never really been laid since the Irishman acted as guide to his ladye's bower. It was all very well to talk, but though, of course, it was like Madge to wish to help Kerry in his need, would she have come so instantly and actually taken up her quarters in his lodgings had there been no warmer feeling than mere kindly interest? And even if she did care for him, it was unfitting, it was unmaidenly—all the more unmaidenly the more she cared—and it was in that way unlike her, though she never thought much of conventionalities. She was old enough to know better ; it was indecent ; it was horrible. His instinct had not at first misled him. There was something he failed to understand between her and Kerry. And then, how could she dream of leaving her father still in his extremity of weakness? Clearly Mr. Serle had not yet reached that perfect state of love which casteth out fear!

' I don't understand it at all,' he said at length, staring moodily at the servant.

' No more don't anybody exactly,' replied

that handmaiden, quite misunderstanding his remark ; 'though the lady she does say she thinks he must have mixed his punch too strong—it was a habit of his, she says, which she warned him about many and many's the time.'

'What!!' exclaimed Selwyn in a whole series of interjections.

'And, indeed, I know myself he had been drinking a good lot,' went on the girl, 'because the decanter and jug were both empty.'

'How did the lady know he had met with an accident?' asked the young man.

'Mr. Kerry gave the doctor her address, and he wrote to her, and she came as fast as ever she could.'

Here was revealed a pretty state of things ! Selwyn could not doubt that what the servant said was true.   Yet how could it ever have come to be true ? After making all allowance for those flowers of rhetoric which adorn and beautify the arid paths of domestic service, how did it happen Madge had spoken to this girl at all on the subject of Mr. Kerry's fondness for the best Irish ?

It seemed incredible to the young man that his reserved, discreet love could have so deteriorated. Association with Mr. Kerry had produced disastrous results indeed! He Selwyn, would not allow such a state of things to continue longer—not for an hour —not for five minutes.

'Ask the lady to speak to me,' he said. 'Stay; here is my card—take it up and beg her to come down at once.'

'Just step in here,' said the servant, opening the dining-room door, 'and I'll tell her.'

Selwyn was only kept waiting a few minutes, yet he had contrived to work himself into a fever of indignation when the door opened and a familiar voice exclaimed :

'Oh! Mr. Serle, and is it indeed you? What a dreadful thing this is!—poor dear Mr. Kerry—the very best of men!' and Miss Dormer applied her handkerchief to her eyes and wept copiously.

Never in his life before had Selwyn experienced such a revulsion of feeling. He was so thankful, so rejoiced, he had much ado to refrain from embracing Miss Dormer, and his greeting was cordial in the extreme.

'I am so glad to see you!' he exclaimed. 'So relieved to know Kerry has such a friend with him. Tell me all about what is the matter. I hope he is not much hurt.'

'But he is,' sobbed Miss Dormer. 'He has broken his arm, and cut his head open and bruised himself terribly.'

'And the servant tells me his ribs are injured—two of them broken, I think she said.'

'The story-telling little hussy!' cried Miss Dormer indignantly; 'things are bad enough, but they are not so bad as all that comes to. It is his head which is troubling us most—and he is *so* excited.'

'How did the accident happen?' asked Selwyn.

'That is what we can't make out. He told the doctor at first that a footstool tripped him up. Poor fellow, do you remember how he used always to kick mine into a corner and say naughty words about them? But now he says something—only I don't mind him much, for he is light-headed very often —about having been speaking ill of the saints, and how he's properly punished for it; and he has promised—I am sure I could not repeat half of what he has promised to his patron, if he'll only mend his arm fast, and let him get out of his bed and go down to the office. It is cruel to hear the way the dear fellow takes on, Mr. Serle—it is indeed.'

'Is there nothing I can do?' asked Selwyn. 'Can't I sit up with him to-night?'

'Oh, Mr. Serle! will you—will you really, for a few hours?'

'Of course I will, and only be too glad; among us we can surely pull him right in a very short time. I have to pay a visit in the neighbourhood; but I will be back again directly, and then you must let me help you in every way you are able to think of, because——' but there he paused.

'Because what?' asked Miss Dormer.

'We must not allow you to get old before your time,' audaciously finished the young man, with a roguish smile; 'if we did Kerry would never forgive us, nor himself, for that matter.'

'Get off with you,' exclaimed Miss Dormer, highly pleased.

CONCLUSION.

WHILE he was lying on what he called the 'broad of his back,' Mr. Kerry found ample leisure for considering how 'the snipe's courtship' might best be brought to a satisfactory conclusion, and at last, after ' he had thought and better thought' matters over, he opened his mind to Selwyn, and showed him the treasures contained therein.

Thanks to good nursing and a sound constitution—which he had never injured by imbibing more than he could help ' of that poison called Scotch whisky' ('You'd better mind what you are about with Irish,' advised the doctor, to whom he made this remark)—Mr. Kerry's recovery was rapid 'once he passed the turning-point,' a point, however, it may be observed, which gave great anxiety to his friends.

'I'm making a mend of it now,' the Surveyor said to Selwyn one Saturday afternoon, when he called and found his friend propped up in an easy-chair, listening most placidly to Miss Dormer, who was, for his benefit, continuing aloud the history of 'The Three Musketeers.'

'She's a beautiful reader,' said Mr. Kerry, when Miss Dormer had, according to custom, modestly retired and left the gentlemen alone. 'You should just hear her go at those French names.'

'Isn't it rather an awkward book to read aloud?' suggested Selwyn, who had a tolerably distinct recollection of some embarrassing passages in the Musketeers' experiences.

'Not at all—what would make it awkward? Sure, if she comes to anything she doesn't like she skips it, turns over a page or two, and goes on again.'

'That spoils the story, though, does it not?'

'Devil a spoil! You shall hear her when she comes back.'

'Thank you, Kerry. I would much rather not,' answered Selwyn ungratefully.

'Well, well, have it as you like; but you never came across a better reader—that I know.'

'You will never be able to do without her, Kerry.'

'You don't know what I can do without,' answered the Surveyor drily; 'but I have nothing to say against Miss Dormer. She's as good a soul as you'd meet with in the length of a summer's day, and if she's not so young as she was once, it's not her fault.'

'I think it is rather an advantage,' returned Selwyn. 'If she had been in her teens, she could not have come here to nurse you.'

'There is something in that,' agreed Mr. Kerry reflectively. He was thinking, however, though Miss Dormer was not in her teens, she seemed to imagine she had taken a risky step when she complied with his request; but he uttered no word of this, only said: 'I'm well pleased you've come here early, because I want to talk to you about your young woman. Give me all your ears, and don't be angering me.'

' I won't if I can help doing so.'

' First and foremost, then, you have not taken other lodgings for them yet ?'

' No, I promised you I would not till you told me : though why you thought it best they should stay where they are I cannot imagine.'

' Well, one reason was that no lodging-house-keeper would have taken in a man as bad as Trosdale was, and another, that I wish you to get married before you make any shift.'

' Married !' repeated Selwyn in amazement.

' Just that ! If you do not get married now maybe you never will. Once Trosdale's about nobody can tell what notion he may take—and you should put it beyond his power to separate you again. I would have you to say no word to anybody. There's a church in the parish where the Trosdales are living —that one in Regent Square—and you could walk out some morning TWO, and walk back ONE, without a bit of trouble. Then you can choose your time to tell the old man. Miss

Dormer, if you like, will go with you, and you would need no one else—beside the clergyman and the clerk.'

'But do you think——' and Selwyn paused.

'Do I think what?'

'Do you believe I should be justified in marrying so soon?'

'I believe you would not be justified in putting your marriage off a day longer than you can help. You've heaps to keep a wife on as you are, and once I'm about I'll see you are put in your right position. You'd have been a Surveyor long ago, but that Dandison put a cross against your name. We'll soon have it off though, if you only do as I bid you.'

'I will if Madge agrees.'

'Madge must agree. The old man ought to go out of town for a while, and you ought to be married before he goes. I have planned it all, and, if you do what I tell you, mice in a cheese won't be better and happier than you and your girl—though she doesn't deserve any luck at all, by reason of her not taking a good offer when it was made to her.'

'She did not show good taste there, Kerry.'

'She showed the worst of taste, and the worst of sense—but that's neither here nor there. I made up my mind the night I nearly ended my days over that cursed stool I was far better without her—or at any rate without her father—and you can no more separate the pair than you could the Siamese twins. A fine handful you'll have with him! Still, if you're pleased I'm sure I may be.'

'I am pleased,' said Selwyn very decidedly.

'Then go and be more pleased. Tell her to be ready, and then walk round and find out from the clerk how soon you can be married.'

'I only hope she may consent.'

'How many times am I to tell you she must consent? See here, if she's contrary, bring her to me; I've a word to say which will bring her to reason.'

'Can't you say it to me? I never am able to persuade her to go out of the house.'

'Humph!' remarked Mr. Kerry, and he sat silent for a little. 'I wonder whether I could write?' he said after that pause.

' I shouldn't try. You are still weak, you know,' urged Selwyn.

' 'Pon my soul, I believe you are still jealous !' mocked Mr. Kerry. ' See, there's pen and ink and paper ; write what I want said for yourself and I'll sign it. You needn't be making any beginning now—any "dears," or the rest of it.'

' What am I to say ?' asked Selwyn, biting the end of his pen.

' You may say, " The last time we had any talk." Have you got that down ?'

' Yes. Go on.'

' " You seemed to think you owed me something." '

' What did she think she owed you ?' asked Selwyn.

' Only a trifle she was in my debt, or thought she was. " If you are still of the same mind, marry Serle at once, and so wipe out all scores." That's all. Hand it over till I sign—no need to say " Yours truly ;" she knows I am "hers truly—Daniel Kerry"—and tell her from me, will you, that fathers always provide their daughters' wedding-dresses, and I'll send her one. I am her father now.

Maybe you didn't know that ? Well, I am. Ask her, and you'll find she'll not deny it.'

* * * * *

Mr. Kerry created quite a sensation when he went down to Somerset House with his left arm in a sling, and asked to see Mr. Tenterden.

'Hallo !' exclaimed that gentleman, when the Surveyor walked in, 'what's all this that has been the matter with you ? I had no idea you were so ill. You look like a ghost.'

'I'm not one though,' answered Mr. Kerry. 'When I am, it is not back here I'll be coming, I hope.'

'You might come to a worse place. Well, what do you want—leave of absence to go out of town ?'

'You are wrong,' answered Mr. Kerry; 'it is nothing about myself I've come for at all. I only want a talk with you concerning an Assistant fellow that has been very badly treated—young Serle.'

'How has he been badly treated ? If it's Serle at Stratford you mean, I have done all I could for him.'

'I want you to think whether you can't do more still. He has had the worst of bad luck since he entered the service. First of all, Dandison sent him to Liverpool, where there wasn't one but myself to teach him a thing.'

'He could not have had a better instructor,' said Mr. Tenterden politely.

'That is as it may be,' replied Mr. Kerry, declining the compliment; 'at any rate, he couldn't have had a worse chief than Trosdale. In a manner of speaking, the poor lad fell among thieves, and, though he was honest and industrious as the day, Dandison took a spite against him, and kept him back from his examination, and played the deuce with his chances.'

'If what you say is correct, Mr. Kerry, the matter shall be put right.'

'What I say is correct, and the matter can't be put right, because he has lost a year clean; but he'll not moan about that if you only rub the black mark off him. And you ought, for he's a decent fellow, and married to as good a girl as you'd find in the three kingdoms.'

'Married—that boy married!' exclaimed Mr. Tenterden, firmly fixing his glass in his eye, and regarding Mr. Kerry through it.

' He's not a boy—he's five-and-twenty past, and I saw him married myself; for the first time the doctor said I might go out I gave the bride away myself. She has a father of her own—old Trosdale—but he's no more good to her than he is to himself.'

' Do you mean to say Serle is married to Trosdale's daughter—to the daughter of the old idiot who commuted his pension and threw the money into a blast furnace ?'

' The very same. He threw every penny into it a man called Ashford left him. It was Ashford got the bulk—said Trosdale owed him the money.'

' Cramsey knew a person called Ashford.'

' Did he though ? Then I see daylight. I have always blessed M'Closky for persuading Dandison to send Cramsey and his laundry away from Liverpool.'

' It was not Dandison—it was I,' said Mr. Tenterden with a modest pride. ' I went down one day and caught him at the wash-tub—in the very act.'

'That's just what Serle did the first day he came to Liverpool—when his misfortunes began.'

'I ought not to say so, I suppose, but I must tell you in confidence I suspect his misfortunes are nearly ended. We will send up for Mr. Harrison, and you must tell him the whole story at more length than you have told it to me. Only the other day he was talking about the Trosdales, and wishing he could find them. He thought he might manage to get Trosdale some light post here.'

'Don't let him do that,' said Mr. Kerry in a tone of earnest entreaty—'for the love of heaven don't let him do that! The only chance for Trosdale and his daughter is for Serle—wherever he is—to have his father-in-law in the office with him, as head clerk you know. He'd do well enough then— could talk to the public, and tell anybody that liked to listen all about his furnace. I have thought it over till my head has ached, and I can see no other plan. I would take him for clerk myself, but he'd never call me " Mr.

Kerry ;" and I could not find it in my heart
to bid a man like him say " Sorr." '

It was too much. Mr. Tenterden burst into
a peal of laughter, in the midst of which
Mr. Harrison entered the room.

' What's all this ?' he asked. ' Tenterden,
I cannot remember to have ever before seen
you so strangely moved.'

' You must ask Mr. Kerry,' answered the
other.

' Mr. Kerry has not a notion what's the
matter with you.' said that gentleman, fairly
mystified ; 'and if I had I wouldn't say
another word, for I am tired out and must
get home, or I'll be laid up again.'

' Yes, you must take care of yourself,'
observed Mr. Tenterden. ' I am heartily
sorry to see you looking so ill.'

'And you can tell Mr. Harrison what I say.
It's about Trosdale I've been talking,' he
added in explanation. ' But I won't talk more
now, for my head is getting bad again, and
besides I don't think there is any need. I
couldn't leave the future of Serle and his
wife in better hands, I am very sure.'

'Indeed you could not,' said Mr. Tenterden earnestly ; adding with conviction, as he closed the door after his visitor, ' There goes the kindest creature I ever met—and the strangest.'

THE END.

BILLING & SONS, PRINTERS, GUILDFORD.

G., C. & Co.